CITY *of* GOD

GIL CUADROS

CITY LIGHTS
SAN FRANCISCO

© 1994 by Gil Cuadros
All Rights Reserved

Cover design & photography by Rex Ray
Book design by Amy Scholder
Typography by Harvest Graphics

"At Risk" first appeared in *Asklepios Journal*, 1990; "RM#," in *Art X Press*, Volume 1, No. 1, 1990; "There are places you don't walk at night, alone," *Harbinger*, 1990; "Sight," in *Blood Whispers 2*, 1994; "Unprotected," in *Indivisible*, 1991; "Indulgences," in *High Risk 2*, 1994.

Library of Congress Cataloging-in-Publication Data

Cuadros, Gil.

City of God / Gil Cuadros.

p. cm.

ISBN 0-87286-295-X : $9.95

1. Hispanic American gays — California — Los Angeles — Literary collections.
2. AIDS (Disease) — Patients — California — Los Angeles — Literary collections.
3. Hispanic American men — California — Los Angeles — Literary collections.
4. Hispanic Americans — California — Los Angeles — Literary collections.
5. Gay men — California — Los Angeles — Literary collections. 6. Los Angeles (Calif.) — Literary collections. I. Title.

PS3553.U22C58 1994
818'.5409 — dc20

94-23225
CIP

CITY LIGHTS BOOKS are edited by Lawrence Ferlinghetti and Nancy J. Peters and published at the City Lights Bookstore, 261 Columbus Avenue, San Francisco, CA 94133.

ACKNOWLEDGEMENTS

At the end of 1987, when my lover John died, I was given two years to live according to my doctor's estimate. Writing literally saved or at least extended my life. Still I couldn't have done it without the guidance and support of my much loved teacher Terry Wolverton. She listened and stood by me in my times of grief and struggle with my diagnosis as well as the joyful times and the little work time we actually had left for writing after sharing in class. Anything to avoid *that writing part.*

My life is doubly blessed with the two most important men in my heart: Marcus Antonio and Kevin Martin.

I'd also like to acknowledge Thom Cardwell and David Hirsch whose meteoric love for each other has inspired my life beyond words.

Furthermore I owe thanks to the Brody Art Foundation and PEN/USA West for their financial support and encouragement. Finally love and light to John-Roger and MSIA, Michael Niemoeller, Paul Attinello, Luis Alfaro and VIVA and Laura Aguilar.

For John Edward Milosch
1952–1987

Contents

1

2

1

INDULGENCES

My mother and father had both come from the same home town, Merced, California. They romanticized the red checkerboard-patterned water tower on J Street, the Purina feed store on K, the old, semi-demolished church that looked like Mexico, rough-hewn, gritty pink stone L Street. Pulling off the highway, my parents would cluck their tongues, stare out of our black Impala, disbelieving the changes. They told my brother and me of the time when blacks kept to their own side of town. "Now the place has gone to pot."

Dad parked at the small grocery store, El Mercado

Merced, a converted house with boarded-up windows and wrought iron bars for protection. The place had a little bit of everything: warped, dark, wooden shelves carrying sodas, tortillas, lard and eggs, things the neighbors always seemed to run out of first. It was central to both sides of my family. Uncle Ruben lived near the corner; Grandma Lupe, across the street; Uncle Cosme, next to her. My great-grandfather Tomas had lived two houses down. "Papa" would walk this street every day, wave to my relatives as he passed by, his blanched wooden cane steadying his balance, the handle dark where he gripped. It was Ruben who went to try to see in the windows why Papa hadn't gone by that day. It was Cosme who called two days ago to tell us Papa was dead.

My little brother and I ached to get out of the car, the long ride had caused our legs to fall asleep. Jess had complained the whole way that I was invading his side; my father turned from his steering: "Do I have to remind you that you are fourteen years old and should just ignore your younger brother?" Dad was already irritated and said he was going to take Jess to Grandma Lupe's. I was to go with my mother. My mother wanted me to mind because someone had died.

"It's out of respect," she warned while she collected the things she needed from the glove box: a mirror, make-up, tissue. And as we walked the short distance down the street, I looked back and saw my father pull a six-pack of beer from the old cooler in front of the *mercado.* His hands dripped melted crushed ice, and the sidewalk became stained with its moisture.

My great-grandfather's house always reminded me of a ranch, the oppressive heat of the San Joaquin Valley, the large wagon wheel leaning against the standing mail box, the way the long, tan, stucco building hugged the ground. I expected tumbleweeds to roll by, a rattlesnake to be coiled seductively in the flower bed's rocks. My mother's cousin, Evelyn, had been taking care of Papa and she met us at the door before we even knocked. My mother had just straightened herself again, licking the tips of her fingers in the driveway, touching up her hair on the porch. Evelyn and my mother fell into each other's arms as soon as they saw each other, making a show of tears, almost religiously. She was the same age as my mother, thirty, maybe a few months apart. I stood awkward on the porch, afraid to walk in unannounced. Evelyn wore a flimsy dress, a brownish print the same color as the house. Her teeth were stained, and when she smiled her long dog teeth poked out. Hair hung down her back like dry weeds.

"Well," she said, facing me, "who is this foxy young man?"

My mother laughed. "This is my oldest boy." Evelyn swung her dress like she was dancing to a *ranchero* tune, showing her kneecaps, and I stared. My mother always wore pants and it was strange, I thought, for a woman to be home in a dress. She wasn't going anywhere.

She tilted her head coyly at me. "Why don't you give

me a big hug. We're family." I put my arms around her like a mechanical claw. She pulled me in tight, placing my face above her breast. I could smell her sweat, a scent of dairy products, cheese and bad milk. It felt like her breast had dampened my face and I wiped away droplets from my cheek. "He looks like your old man, Lorraine." My mother acknowledged this standing near a cabinet filled with ceramic salt and pepper shakers, ashtrays from Vegas, Tahoe, and the biggest little city, Reno. Mom had confided to me she wanted something to remember Papa by.

My mother said, "I just came over, Evelyn, to see where it happened." She held a ceramic Siamese cat with an ear broken off and holes bored in its head.

Evelyn explained that she had come home late from work, she had found him in the bathroom, collapsed, a green mess pooled underneath him. She said, "He started having trouble, not making it in time, then I'd have to clean it up. Sometimes he'd lose it just sleeping in his chair. I told your mother, Lorraine, that he should go into a home. No one wanted to hear about it. I couldn't take care of him twenty-four hours a day."

My mother started to cry again and walked over to see the bathroom, a tissue covering her nose and mouth. I stood with Evelyn. I had heard so many stories about her, how she was dropped from the crib, how soft and impressionable the skull is at that age. My aunts would start low and sympathetic, how it wasn't Evelyn's fault for the way it was with her, but then would tell each other what a tramp, a slut Evelyn had become. They'd snicker about how she slept with black men, white men. Papa should have put her away. Evelyn's Papa's angel. Evelyn's a lesbian.

Evelyn smiled at me. I looked around the living room, touched the lamps made out of thick coiled ropes, burlap shades. Evelyn lit a cigarette, clicked shut the silver-toned Zippo lighter. "Do you have a girlfriend?"

"No, not really," I answered.

I felt embarrassed. My whole family was always asking when was I going to get a girlfriend. My mother begged me to find a girl soon, not to be so shy, said it was natural for me to like girls. She'd say she worries because she's a mother, don't you want to make your father proud, your brother should look up to you. The truth was I had a lot of friends who were girls. They would pass notes with me in class, short-lined confessions of love for some other boy. Their reasons for love were always the same: the color of eyes, the length of hair, the muscles sneaking out from the boys' short-sleeved shirts. These same boys would shove me around before the bus came. My body would grow warm and my heart would pound when they put their hands on my chest and shoulders. I would notice the color of their eyes, the strength they possessed. "Fucking sissy," they would say and then give me one good last punch.

Evelyn seemed like she couldn't believe I wouldn't have a girlfriend. "Oh, then you like someone. What's her name?" I squirmed that I didn't like anyone and no one liked me. She offered me a sip of her soda, it fizzed in a glass, water had ringed the wood coffee table.

"No, thank you," I said.

"Oooh, you're so polite. Why don't you sit next to me." I came over to the Afghan-covered couch where she sat. I could hear my mother's sobs, the bathroom becoming an echo chamber. Evelyn moved close to me on the couch. "I bet you kiss like a stud," she said. She put her hand on my knee and I started to feel a horrible warmth between my legs, growing. She squeezed my thigh as if to make me laugh, then asked, "What do you do for fun?"

I stumbled as I stood up, fell back down. "I go to the Scouts," I offered, hoping the conversation would end and my mother would re-enter the scene, grab me by the wrist and take me away.

Evelyn looked deep in my eyes, as if to devour a creamy pastry. "Will you do me a favor?" she asked. I nodded, hoping it would involve leaving. "Will you kiss me?" I pulled back but she came forward and vise-gripped my head. Her other hand reached down and grabbed my dick, her nails digging into the khaki material of my pants. I wanted to vomit, her breath was like my father's, unclean, like a whole night of beer. I shoved her hand off my lap and got up. I licked the sleeve of my shirt, trying to get out the taste of her. She started to laugh as I unlocked the door. The brightness of outside kicked in my allergies and I started to sneeze as I ran to Grandma Lupe's house, saying out loud,

"Forget my mother." My father sat on the steps drinking his Miller's. He tried to grab onto my butt as I passed him. I let the screen door slam behind me and ran for the nearest bathroom, Grandma Lupe's. I barely made it before I puked. From inside I could hear my grandma talking on the phone saying Evelyn should have been locked up a long time ago. My head hung over the tub's edge, water rushing down the drain. The porcelain reeked of Calgon and Efferdent.

Tension and humidity hung in the old house. Relatives were arriving every moment; my grandmother was wringing her hands. My mother was still crying that she couldn't depend on anyone: my brother, too young; my father, always drinking; and me, worthless. I was too embarrassed to tell her why I had run out of Evelyn's and had decided to hide out in the backyard. I was surprised that my mother had come to get me. My brother and I were playing in the old rickety garage filled with an ancient white Chevy on blocks, wooden barrels of pecans and walnuts in the dark back corner.

My mother wanted me at the kitchen table with all my aunts and my mother's aunts. I was the only boy except for two *viejos*, my mother's uncles, both too old to decline the meeting. My mother said, "You are family. You need to hear."

My grandmother Mikala sat at the center of the long kitchen table; she mirrored the Last Supper needlepoint that hung, framed, above her head. Grandma

Mickey's face was near-silhouette because of the big open windows behind her. Jars of *nopales* glittered in the pantry. Cactus grew along the fence outside and guarded this secret meeting. Just as my mother would light up at the onset of a long story, Mickey smoked a Newport. She exhaled a large burst of smoke. "As you know, I went to the police. Papa had horrible bruises on his body, especially on his hand, like someone had kept on slamming the door on his wrist. I think Evelyn killed him, made him have a heart attack. The bruises on his hand were ugly."

Around the table, aunts and cousins shook their heads, each taking turns. "Evelyn has always been crazy. She was spoiled rotten by Papa. He never saw how evil she was. He always gave her dresses and toys, didn't give anything to us kids."

Grandma Mickey raised her open palms. "I will make her pay, I swear." I felt sickened that a murderess had kissed me that day and I wanted to interrupt Mickey, to tell her Evelyn had grabbed between my legs. Mom made me put my hand down, kept it hidden below the table, squeezing my fingers occasionally.

My mother's Uncle Ruben spoke. "It's all our own faults, we should have never left him alone with her. Mikala, you should have taken him instead of leaving him with that crazy prostitute. And where is Evelyn's mother? Mary is always gone, never responsible. *Hijo!* It was bad enough Papa had to take Evelyn in and raise her, just because Mary didn't want her child in an institution."

Mikala again raised her palms. "It would kill Mary to know her own girl killed Papa." There was argument all around the table about what to do, then dinner was passed, refried beans, peppered steak, home-made tortillas, Pepsi taken out dusty from the cellar. We all ate with gusto, ready to stone Evelyn. I held my secret, knowing it wasn't important. All around me people were saying, "Eat Gilberto, eat."

I had never been to a wake before, the orange and purple summer night having just started, the air extremely dry. I could make out bats flying against the sunset. My Grandma Mickey and all her sisters were behind dark netting, a special section for the immediate family. From behind the curtain, I could hear their sobbing. My mother whispered to my father that Evelyn was inside and it wasn't fair, none of the other cousins were there. My father sighed, uninterested. I pretended to be appropriately mournful since I'd never seen a dead body before. It lay in its open coffin, a spotlight illuminating his pasty face, like a stage actor, I thought. My mother huffed, "It makes me sick, you can hear her going on and on."

My father said, hot-tempered, "She has a right to her grief."

My mother turned into quick anger, "You know what I mean, Danny. You heard what my mother said."

Exasperated, my father whispered sideways, "You have no proof."

"The bruises, Danny, the bruises," my mother near spat till my father said, "Shh!" In the quiet before the wake, I could easily make out Evelyn's wails. They were the kind of wails that could be mistaken for laughing, as if this were all a joke and my great-grandfather would pop up then and yell, "We pulled a fast one on all of you!"

I thumbed through the small book given to me as I had entered the mortuary, *How to say the Rosary Apostolic and Other Indulgences.* Grandma Mickey said it was a gift for me: "The mysteries are great and powerful for the devout; the joyful, sorrowful and glorious acts of Jesus purify our sins." It was pretty boring stuff, fifteen Our Fathers and one hundred and fifty Hail Marys. The pictures made it seem more exciting.

After the wake, uncles, aunts, grandparents and children waited on the steps of the mortuary, leaning against the colonnades. An aunt kicked a strip of no-slip on a step with the point of her shoe, her husband held his jacket over his arm, his short-sleeved shirt exposing his various tattoos of roses and crosses. Another man with a full black mustache that covered his mouth's expression spoke with him. Aunt Mary had been hastily escorted out by her youngest daughter. Evelyn stood by the coffin long after everyone had left. "Nearly threw herself on top," an uncle said. Everyone had moved their cars so they blocked all the exits, the headlights aimed for the front door, the marble walls, the angels and muscular men along the frieze. Ruben called out, "She's coming."

When Evelyn walked outside all the car lights' high beams were turned on. The women and men stepped away from their cars, toward Evelyn. They began yelling, "Get out of here! We know you did it. You murdered Papa. Sick, sick, sick!" Evelyn had been covering her eyes, trying to see, to adjust. She wore an open black crocheted top and the headlights bore through to flesh, bounced off the black Qiana dress as if it were made of white.

She started to scream, to reason, "I didn't do it." I wondered why she didn't just run or why one of my uncles didn't put a stop to this, their barrel chests filled with breath, their shirts almost too tight, their top buttons aching to pop. But they wouldn't. She tried to block her eyes with her hands, shaking her head, "He always shitted on himself." Horns blared, hands heavy on steering wheels; my brother leaned on ours from the back seat, our father having rushed us in early. My Grandmother Mikala walked up to Evelyn and began to slap her, nails curled to puncture, looking fierce. Evelyn defended herself, thrust herself like a cat, wild and rare, on top of my grandmother; both fell dangerously down the steps, backs, spines, shoulder blades hitting the corners. People rushed in like a mob, women pulling her hair, kicking Evelyn in the stomach, the ass, her breast. The men tried, some laughing, to extract their wives from the brawl. My brother and I jumped up and down in the back seat, acted as if we could feel the blows or were giving them, vocalized the sound of each good hit, "uhh, opff." We watched as Dad returned with my mother, who was nearly scratching his eyes out, saying loudly, "That bitch."

My father hastily drove away to his mother's house, it now fully night. My mother told me to forget what had happened, that it wasn't a good thing, that she was already feeling ashamed, her voice quiet and firm. She thought that maybe I should pray. My little brother was asleep already, his straight black hair next to my thigh. I rolled the window down slightly, letting the air rush in. I could barely hear the radio, a scatter of signals. I stared outside, wondered if my family would ever turn on me, where would I go, who would I love. The long farm roads leading back greeted my thoughts, the rows of grapevines, tomato furrows, cotton, all lined up in parallel paths ending on the horizon, designed like manifest destiny. Lit by my father's high beams, still ignited, I watched as we passed a scarecrow off the road, dry weeds for hair, a flimsy brown dress, a stake skewered up through the body, arms stretched open as if ready to embrace.

REYNALDO

It was the last month of summer, August dwindling down to a few weeks, drying up like water on the hot driveway. The family's new 1970 Corvair was freshly washed. Reynaldo wished the days would not go by so quickly, wished he could spend what remained under his family's large avocado tree in the backyard, chasing his shadow around the trunk, his mother would say. In a few weeks he'd be attending a new school, a school for older kids. He wondered if they would like him, if the teachers would be just as nice as his own Mr. Lloyd or Mr. Palmer.

Grandma is going to die soon. She broke her hip, lost her sight. Cancer runs through her body as if just the thought could make it real. It would have come sooner if it weren't for the miracle of medicines. Now there's nothing to be done except feed her mild pain pills and change her diapers. Mom and Dad have asked me to take care of her. They say since I have experience with medical situations, I know what to do. It has been years since I last saw her. My brother warns me that I'll feel bad if I don't go. My therapist thinks a journal will be good for me, something to go back to when this is all over, a place to process all that is going on.

Reynaldo's mother often warned him of his day-dreaming under the tree, and set him to task if she found him curled up near the trunk. The roots spread open like two hands cradling him; beneath him clover spread like a blanket thrown open for a picnic. His mother whispered his name, touching Reynaldo's shoulder. She told him that they were driving up to his grandmother's house, that his father had taken time off from work so that he could take Reynaldo fishing, play catch, and barbeque.

She went blind first from a bad operation. No one seemed to care enough to sue the doctor. I had my own reasons for not getting involved: that I wouldn't be around to see the trial end, that it would have a bad effect on my own health. Now Mom tells me,

"Grandma, she's tired of living." What I don't say is, we don't get tired of living, we get tired of the pain.

I've tried to make death a friend.

The drive was long, his mother and father taking turns at the wheel, the road twisting through the string of mountains called the Grapevine. Reynaldo always knew they were near when their car would be free of all the curves in the road and his ears would pop from the altitude. Below he could see the borders of the highway covered in golden poppies all the way to what seemed like the edge of the world. His Grandma Rosario lived in the country next to a strawberry field and an orchard of peaches and apricots. A train ran by the rickety, two-story house and shook the floor and walls, rattling the small statues of Saint Gerome and Saint Francis.

My aunt washes Grandma everyday, but Grandma still smells sour. Nobody can fix her hair right, her hair as long as a young girl's. The women in my family have threatened to cut grandma's hair short, divide up the strands among them, tie ribbons to the ends.

I've brought few things with me, a tape player with recorded meditations, small photographs, pills and some astragalus and echinacea. It's hard to keep track of my pills and the times I need to take them; I'm forgetful.

I went exploring in the attic the other day. My aunt

was bathing Grandma. I found a small diary, mildewed and water-stained with postcards from Europe inside.

My father said I ought to stake my claim before the rest of the family starts horning in.

Reynaldo knew as sure as the sun and the moon that Grandma would have food ready for his family when they arrived. As he walked through the front door he could already smell the fresh-cooked beans, a waft of peppered steak and homemade tortillas. Grandma Rosario set the last plate down for the feast, then turned around to give Reynaldo a big hug and kiss. It made Reynaldo giggle, her tiny hands tickling his side, her nose rubbing his ear. Even while he was laughing he heard a strange sound, something he could not place, like money jingling in a bag or it might even have been someone singing.

There are times I want to tell Grandma what's wrong with me and that I want her to say hello to my lovers in heaven, but she can't even tell I am there in the room watching her. Voices pop in my head. I hear the clock strain to make the next second. I crack open the old black diary I found; pages slip off the spine and onto the floor, as if forgettable.

July 10, 1923

Dear Jesus,

I'm addressing this diary to you because of the feelings we share. Please forgive my tirades the other day, I hardly know what possessed me to cry like that, then to turn on you, spitting venomous words that were sure to hurt. The accusations about her were really uncalled for on my part, I'm sure she's a handsome woman.

I guess it's because the end is coming near, but then again new days start almost as soon. Let me tell you also that I'm writing a song in your honor.

Your Dearest Friend

The meal was delicious and Reynaldo couldn't believe that they were going to have ice cream next. Grandma Rosario spooned out huge scoops of chocolate, vanilla and strawberry, all the while Reynaldo hearing the strange sound of coins banging against each other. He shook his head, stuck his fingers in his ears to clear them out, to make sure he was hearing right. He turned to his mom. "What is that?" "What's what?" she asked. Reynaldo faced his father. "What's that weird noise?" His father shrugged his shoulders. "Beats me," was all he could offer, his mouth filled with soft vanilla ice cream. Grandma Rosario sat down next to Reynaldo with her bowl. "Grandma," Reynaldo asked, "what's that funny noise?" The sound of coins filled his ears again, this time accompanied by a singing voice, but Reynaldo couldn't make out the words. "Maybe the train's coming," his grandma said, thoughtfully, "then again, it could be my friend the ghost." "The ghost!" Reynaldo shrieked. "Well, he's not really my friend. I can't believe your father hasn't told you about the ghost." His father just smiled, taking another large scoop of ice cream. Reynaldo's eyes bugged out. Shaking his head, he said, No, Grandma, Dad didn't tell me anything. "We only became friends because he stays on his side of the house and I stay on mine, that's why the attic's closed. He lives up there, sings a bit loudly some nights, but all in all it's rather pleasant. I imagine he's very good looking, and has a real high voice."

Aunts and uncles have been coming over a lot this week. Some even have nerve enough to ask me if they can take this or that home already. They are sure Grandma wouldn't mind. An aunt asked how I was doing, my face gaunt and arms slender. She warned me not to go into the attic. My uncle had lost his eye there, a nail had come flying out of the wall when he was young. I had already placed the bronze clock in the trunk of my car and a framed photograph of my grandma and grandpa is hidden in a pocket of my suitcase. My mother said she will call back. She was trying to remember what Grandma had that she'd want. The diary and postcards were displayed on the bureau I used proudly, my aunts and uncles would never want such junk. The small bedroom's scent had changed with these artifacts.

July 18, 1923

Dear Jesus,

I have come up with a fabulous idea. To show my appreciation, I have taken your first name as my own middle name. It's as if we are cousins. I have been studying French diligently every night, so I sign off . . .

A bientot mon cousin

Reynaldo slipped into the sheets of the fold-out sofa, his mother occupying the small extra bedroom, while his father snored wildly next to him. His father's body, the girth and temperature of a water heater, had already warmed up half the bed, but Reynaldo's side was still cool. The room was a bit chilly, and his grandma threw another blanket over her two boys. She gave Reynaldo a small kiss and reminded him to say his prayers before he fell asleep. With that, she switched the light off and the room went black as if Reynaldo were blindfolded or swimming in a pan of motor oil. He got out of bed, knelt and began praying, for his parents, his grandma, his teachers Mr. Lloyd and Mr. Palmer, and his new school. When Reynaldo finished, he could make out most of the room, the bookcase filled with silver-framed photographs of his grandfather who had made this house with his own hands and had gone away not long after Reynaldo was born. His parents would show him pictures of his grandfather, but Reynaldo could never remember him. On the table next to where he lay was a bronze clock shaped like a six-horse stagecoach. The face glowed green, it even colored Reynaldo's hand as he reached over to the tiny whip the driver used to bore down on the team, hooves kicking up dirt, their faces pulled in determination. It was just past eleven.

I had to go home for a few days. Mom took over my vigil. The doctor handed me ten new prescriptions when I came in. Some of my medications need to be taken with food, others not; four of them three times a day, three others twice a day, two every other day, and one, one time a day. Then the doctor asked how I was doing emotionally. I explained the stuff going on in my head, the same words my folks said when I was young when they were mad at me, turning over and over again. He wrote out another prescription, an anti-depressant, then, a mood elevator. He was absolutely sure I was suffering from depression. I shoved the twelve white sheets of paper, each with a different savior and my doctor's signature, into the old diary. I carry it everywhere.

July 27, 1923

Dear Jesus,

Watched you as you walked from store to store. What could you be doing in town, I thought, and going from store to store? As you know, my birthday is coming up and this year I've decided (and yes I know my birthday has always been one of my two favorite holidays, the other Christmas) that we could celebrate simply, just you and me.

au revoir

Reynaldo didn't know how long he had slept, but it was still dark. The statues of Saint Gerome and Saint Francis glowed as if made of the same paint used on the clock's face. He could make out the stairs that led up to the attic. The moon must have been right outside the front door because the light made every step shine, the wood polished until it shone like glass. For some reason, he found it hard to fall asleep; a song seemed to be stuck in his mind and all he could do was hum the melody. Staring at the steps, just about to close his eyes, he suddenly could see coins rolling down the stairs like a waterfall. The noise should have been loud enough to wake his parents, each coin spinning on its side till slowly it lost its momentum. His father moved over, his breathing soft and steady. Reynaldo got up and walked over to the nearest coin. He picked up what seemed like gold, the moon also reflecting on the face of the coin. At first he thought it was a woman, a goddess, but, looking closer he discovered it was a man with delicate features and a nose shaped like his father's, an eagle's profile. As he went to gather the rest of the coins, Reynaldo could hear someone on the top of the stairs, a voice singing in Spanish, "*Mi amore, desvanecer.*" "My love" was all that Reynaldo could understand, but the man who glowed, whose garments flowed in no wind, made Reynaldo run in terror, his heart in his throat. He shook his father till he woke up. "What, what?" "I saw the ghost, Dad. Wake up, he's coming down the stairs." "Go back to bed, *Mijo,* it's just a dream you had." Reynaldo looked behind him; now he could barely make out the stairs, the moon had gone away, the coins had disappeared, all except the one he held tightly in his palm, and he wasn't sure it would not vanish too.

No one at Grandma's asked where I had gone or said a word to me, except to tell me I lost too much weight, that I was skinny. My aunt was upset that I left my grandmother "at this hour." She then said I wasn't needed today. I went to the only gay bar in town. This was a real dive, with fake wood paneling, a pool table and piano. This authentic-looking Mexican guy came up to me. He wasn't very tall, I thought, since I was sitting down and I was still half a head above him. He asked where I lived. I told him I wasn't interested. He walked away, a little embarrassed because some friends of his were watching.

Later when I had to take a leak, he came up to the urinal next to mine. He said, "I live right near here — if you just let me suck you off, you just have to lie back." I guess I acted a bit haughty and he came up to me and started to try to kiss me. He could only reach my neck. "Dammit," I said, "I don't want you. Just leave me alone. I have AIDS, asshole!" The man looked shocked, all he could say was, "You look so good." I started to cry when he left, wondered why I had all the luck.

July 31,1923

Dear Jesus,

My mother wonders when you'll come around again. She was surprised not to see you, she had made a cake and set candles into rosettes made of frosting. It was lovely.

R.J.

Grandma Rosario knelt in a bed of roses, her gardening hat large and white like a halo. The small yard was dominated by roses of every kind, some bushes not much taller than Reynaldo himself, others gigantic, arching above from fence to fence, creating shade from the living canopy. Reynaldo raked with much care around each bush, cautious not to break any of the roses' stems or get pricked by thorns. As soon as he finished, he placed the rake with the other gardening tools, and ran to show his grandma what he found.

"Look, Grandma, look at the coin I found last night." Grandma Rosario let Reynaldo place the coin in her hand. She flipped the coin over and over, looking at the date, the face of the coin as if she was recognizing something that was lost long ago. "It's beautiful, *Mijo.* Where did you find it?" Reynaldo told his grandma of the light from the moon, the sound the coins made rolling down the stairs, and the strange man who sang in Spanish. "Is that your friend the ghost, Grandma?" Reynaldo asked. His Grandma Rosario wouldn't answer, stared at the coin, unable to move or close her eyes.

Grandma wants to get out of bed, but she can't. I hold her down until what little strength she has leaves. She is too heavy to lift herself and she cries.

I go to pick up my dark suit from the cleaners before she passes on. I am sure my folks will not be impressed with this suit, unable to believe I would spend the money to shop at Robinson's and have a tailor. If they should say anything, I'll retort, "You can't be a modern queer today without owning one good dark suit."

She passed on quietly this morning, no one was in the room with her. I had gone to lie down. I had noticed her chest heaving a little. Days ago, the doctor said it was going to be soon. I thought she'd make it through the week, I didn't think it would be today. My aunt was crying my name and I came running in a little dizzy. She

asked, "Where were you, where?" I knew she had wanted me to keep Grandma alive somehow, or, at least hold Grandma's hand till she arrived. I covered her face with the crochet blanket, parts of her flesh showing through the spaces of yarn. My aunt ripped away the blanket in disbelief.

August 1, 1923

Dear Jesus,

How could I ever stay mad at you? And see you show up the very next day, ready to go to the lake for a picnic? It's quite understandable that with all your time spent working you had forgotten my birthday. We will have a considerable amount of money when we get to Europe. I'll never forget the time we have spent and will spend together, Jesus, it's like we are meant to be friends forever.

Today I was at the library searching for places that we could go to that are economical. How does Turkey sound to you? We can visit the Blue Mosque. Or what about India, there are so many temples and ruins of ancient religions. We can both bathe in the Ganges river, or walk on hot coals.

Eternal Love, R.J.

That night was still hot, like it had been all day. Even under the shade, Reynaldo sat with his grandma on the small bench, drinking iced tea with lemon, the roses humming with small bees. Reynaldo's father said he could sleep in his swimming trunks tonight instead of his pajamas. With that his father crashed into dreams, covered by one thin sheet. Reynaldo said his prayers quickly, adding the ghost at the end, wishing that he could somehow meet the ghost and that the ghost could take Reynaldo anywhere in the world with the sweep of his arm: Paris, Vienna, New York City. He kept the coin that had fascinated Grandma Rosario inside his fist all day, then tucked it under his pillow. He closed his eyes for what seemed like only a moment, his grip on the coin loosening. When he opened his eyes, the ghost stood at his bed, with a look on his face just like his grandmother's this afternoon. At first Reynaldo was scared to move, but as he looked deeper into the ghost's face, he could tell there was something caring and gentle in his eyes. Reynaldo ventured, "What's your name?" The ghost smiled, said, "You look like your grandfather did when he was your age." Reynaldo got onto his knees, and the springs of the sofa cried. He went to touch the glowing face of the ghost, dressed in an old-fashioned suit with a large white scarf around his neck that seemed to catch a wind Reynaldo could not feel. The ghost moved away. Reynaldo offered his name instead, "I'm named after my grandfather." The ghost seemed amused. "Actually, your grandfather's name was Jesus. Reynaldo was his middle name." "How do you know that?" Reynaldo asked incredulously. "Come over here," the ghost said. "Look inside this frame, you will see that I'm right." It was a very old photograph of his grandmother and his grandfather. "Go ahead, open it up," the ghost coaxed. Reynaldo slipped off the back, and pulled out the cardboard covered in velvet. From the back, Reynaldo could see that his grandmother had folded the photograph over so that it could fit in this frame. There was a young man on the hidden side of the photograph, dressed like the ghost, his arm around his grandfather's waist. Also on the back of the photograph were names written in a style Reynaldo knew wasn't his grandmother's. "Reynaldo, Jesus, Rosario." His grandfather stood in the middle, and the name in the middle was Jesus. Reynaldo turned to the ghost. "Are you Reynaldo, too?" The ghost nodded an affirmation. "Your grandfather took Reynaldo as his middle name. I took your grandfather's name as my middle name also. He was Jesus Reynaldo and I was Reynaldo Jesus, we were the best of friends, since we were children of your age." "Why are you here?" Reynaldo asked. "Do you want your coin back?" "Keep the coin, Reynaldo, it was meant for your grandfather and you look so much like him. Maybe later I will tell you about him." "And you, too?" Reynaldo slipped in. "And me, too," the ghost echoed.

This morning I woke up so tired. A stream of gray mucus came running out of my nose. It felt like I had pneumonia again. I had shortness of breath. I haven't been eating well and my neck is stiff. Everyone has noticed my weight loss. My family is curious but is too polite to ask directly. The funeral for Grandma is in two days. This is the fourth funeral I've been to this year. I called my therapist, who suggested I miss this

one. Maybe I'll skip the funeral and just write in my journal all day. I need to catch up.

Instead of getting out of bed (trying to avoid the family coming in and out of Grandma's house) I watched a TV program. There was an actor who played an AIDS victim, that was his title in the credit. He wondered if he was going to be around the next year. So he was buying Christmas presents early for everyone in his family (who were all so supportive). He also said his lover died the year before. My own family didn't show up to my last lover's funeral.

August 31, 1923

Dear Jesus,

It's time for me to go. I truly wish to understand your reasons for staying. I can't live here anymore. I hope your home is a beautiful one. When I return for a visit, will you allow me to sleep in your home? I hope so. When you finish the front porch, facing the sunset, please think of me in exotic lands...then again, you can always join me.

Bon soir, R.J.

The days and nights went by so quickly — helping his grandma garden, fishing with his dad — even though he didn't like digging for worms in the morning or hooking them on the boat. Nights were reserved for his communion with the ghost, whom Reynaldo never mentioned to his parents. The ghost told him about times when his grandfather would sneak away from school to go swimming in a nearby pond, or when the ghost and his grandfather bumped heads going down simultaneously to tie their shoes. Reynaldo wanted to know about the coins, and why he sings and jingles money every night. The ghost began another story, "When your grandfather and I were becoming men, we had to get jobs to earn our keep. Our own fathers demanded it. Your grandfather and I saved almost every dollar we made, picking cotton, tomatoes, and peaches so large that if you took a bite out of them, they'd drench your chin. When school had ended, each of us had quite a bit of money. We had always talked about taking this money and living out our dreams, but when the time came, we realized that our dreams were different. I wanted to travel around the world, to see the pyramids, the Great Wall, the bustle of New York. Your grandfather also wanted to do that, but he tempered his desire by owning a large home with a flower garden. So off I went, alone, to see beautiful sights and hear languages, but sadly Jesus did not come along. It was many years later that I wanted to return; I had been living everywhere else but home. When I came to your grandfather's house, I couldn't believe how lovely it was, trellises covered in bougainvilleas, morning-glories, sweet peas, the sections of stained glass in the windows now long since shattered. When the door opened, your grandmother Rosario stood there. She had recognized me as one of Jesus' old friends she hadn't liked. She told me Reynaldo was not home, and would not be coming home this evening. He had gone to help a friend save his orange grove, she said, from the frost-laden night. Her face was stern, as if my presence sullied her floors. I wanted to leave a note, but I was afraid she'd read it or never give it to Jesus. Surely I thought he could never leave this house and his wife. While I was traveling, I had accumulated a bit more money, enough to take your grandfather with me. This bag of gold dollars is what I would have brought him."

There was an utter sadness in the ghost's eyes that Reynaldo could see and it made Reynaldo wish that the ghost were solid like he, that he could put his arms around the ghost's neck and squeeze, to let the ghost know he would always be his friend.

September 15, 1923

Dearest Jesus,

Isn't this postcard lovely. Well, Europe accepts me as one of her children, it is beautiful. I arrived a week ago and found a wonderful room. The woman who runs the place cooks two meals a day for the other tenants and me. I've decided to take up painting.

My mother says she wants to visit me soon. I wonder if you'll ever change your mind on coming. I can see it now, I'll be sitting at a small cafe table, drinking coffee. I can hear you call my name aloud, from the front of my home, "Reynaldo, I'm here, I'm here!"

Please write soon Jesus.

R.J.

The ghost seemed to vanish sooner and sooner during his visits with Reynaldo. And Reynaldo knew that the time was coming when he'd have to go home; his new school would be starting. Reynaldo told the ghost that he was afraid to go to the new school, that the older kids might beat him up, that they might tease him, that his teacher might not like him very much. The ghost let him in on a little secret. He said, "As long as you are fair to people, as long as you accept them for who they are, there will always be people who will love you. If you are unkind, and say mean things to others, it will come back to you, there will be no one for you to love." The ghost stood crying or, Reynaldo thought, it might have been laughing. He unwrapped the silk scarf around his neck and presented it to Reynaldo. It glimmered in Reynaldo's hands. The ghost smiled and began to sing "*Mi amore, desvanecer.*" With that the ghost was gone.

Dad drove me home shortly after the funeral, worried I couldn't make it home safely. My head was splitting, one eye totally blurred from all the coughing. We went straight to the hospital. My fears were realized. They found that I had pneumonia for the third time and probably meningitis of some sort; my neck bent down from the pain. The doctor blames me for it, says I haven't taken good care of myself or followed his instructions. He believes I really want to die. All the while my mother tells her friends and relatives after the funeral that I have inoperable cancer. It makes it easier for her, she says.

November 23, 1923

Dearest Jesus,

Mother has written me saying you'll be marrying soon. I wish you and your bride the best for your life together, but I hope this changes nothing between us. Do I still have a room in your home?

Please write soon.

Friends always, R.J.

Reynaldo's new school started. Wearing the scarf made him a little nervous. He worried if the other students would laugh at him, at the delicate material flying around his neck from the softest breeze. He wondered why no one said anything about his beautiful scarf, except two teachers, Mr. Rodrigues and Mr. Carnes, who mentioned it on the first morning. It seemed that whenever he wore the scarf he would make a friend, a very nice friend like Tommy, Victor, Leonard, and even Tyler and James, the twins. Making friends became so nice that he forgot he always had the scarf tied around his neck. He suspected no one else could see it, though Mr. Rodrigues called it diaphanous.

Reynaldo felt like time flew by so quickly. It was not long after that his father started telling Reynaldo, "Young man, get a job!" The day before his college graduation, Reynaldo looked for a lost button from his shirt. Buried in his closet was a small bank, a tin can with pictures of the Eiffel Tower, the Sphinx, the Empire State Building. He opened the can. Inside, at least a hundred gold coins shimmered. A yellowed note partially obscured by the coins said, "For you and your good friend." Reynaldo showed his family, who were ecstatic, but couldn't for the life of them figure out who left that gift for Reynaldo. The note was signed, R.J.

This will be my last entry (yeah!) from the hospital. I hate whining. I know I will get better at home. I am filled with love for myself. Healing will begin. I draw hearts with colored markers, then branches leading away. In the center I write "I am loved," and on each branch I give an example: because I am a creation of God, because I have a loving family, because I've created loving relationships, and so on. It doesn't matter if it's not true, as long as I believe it is.

I found a letter in the binding of the old diary written in my grandmother's writing. The sheet of paper was so fragile, like an old brown leaf, it came apart in my hand.

July 22, 1962

Dear Reynaldo,

It's like I've known you for all these years, and yet sadly when I write you for the very first time I bring only bad news. Jesus, your very good friend from home, died just a month ago. Cancer attacked his legs first. He then fell into a coma that no one could wake him from. I had always known of your special friendship with my husband, and during his hospital stays I thought of trying to reach you. Admittedly I was a bit jealous of you, but no longer. I know Jesus missed having you near, and he always wished for you to visit and see his family. Jesus and I have grown children. There will always be a room for you at our home.

I also want you to know that I cherish this very special connection of ours, this man who touched both our lives. I would very much like to keep Jesus's memory alive, and you along with him, so we've named our grandson Reynaldo, after you. Please keep in the best of health.

Rosario

CHIVALRY

When I turned nine, my relatives thought there must be something genetically wrong with me, some inherent defect in their first-born sons. My cousin Rolando, crib death. My cousin David, "half-retarded." Me, they couldn't put their finger on it. They were annoyed whenever I spoke, and they thought I whispered intentionally, kept things hidden. And then one day I cut my wrists.

Every Easter my Grandma Lupe would pray novenas for David and me. I would receive a letter from her with a charcoal drawing of Jesus at Gethsemane, and a note saying a novena had been prayed for me. When I was younger, she'd send along five dollars, folded in tissue. My mother fussed and said, "Your grandma isn't rich, you should be very grateful to her." When I turned nine, a week before Easter, I cut my wrists. Then she sent twenty dollars and a bronze medallion of St. Christopher. My mother called her and made arrangements for me to visit during the summer for the month.

It was my second near-death experience. The first had been a near-drowning the year before. Grandma had then sent ten dollars with a novena. It was an incident I couldn't explain. Near where my family was having a reunion, I suddenly found myself underwater. My feet were tied in fishing line and algae at the lake's bottom. The story of cutting myself was similar; my wrists were bleeding, my arms were outstretched, and I had no idea how it started. I tried to explain to my folks, "I was taking out the trash and . . ." Both looked in horror as I came through the kitchen door, my father leaving for work on the night shift. My mother could only say "Aye!" as she grabbed kitchen towels to hold my blood in. My father sat back in a chair and said, "You won't be satisfied until you're dead."

My grandma lived with my Uncle Steve and Tia Gloria off the highway near Delano. They shared a small farm with four other families. My uncle looked like my father only thinner, the back of his neck wrinkled and dark. He worked for Del Monte fixing machines, conveyor belts, and irrigation systems.

Sometimes my cousin David worked there, during canning season, throwing bad fruit off the line, taking home a crate of bruised peaches or tomatoes and a few extra dollars. Grandma would pack bean burritos for his lunch. It was simple work for him, the family said. Driving me up, Uncle Steve said few words, used hand gestures to say, "Can you move the side mirror to the left?" Their driveway had a gravel embankment that didn't allow for a surprise visit, small rocks banged off tires and into the truck's sidewalls. David jumped up and down, his tall thin body spinning around when he saw us drive up. His father sucked in his breath, a tinge of disgust that his fourteen-year-old would act like this. My uncle tried to shoo David away from the truck, yelling out the window, "What did I tell you, David, just what did I tell you?" The front yard was fenced in with tall white-washed planks, on top, weather vanes of all kinds spun from the traffic's wind. On the other side of the highway, tracks ran through a field of wheat grass and barbed-wire fences. As I got out of the cab, David kissed me on the cheek, spun me in his embrace. I let out a nervous laugh. He was the only one I would let do this.

David rambled on about how he caught a ton of pollywogs in the stream nearby. "We can go tomorrow." And that we could sleep in the farmhouse all summer and there was the lake. You can grab sun fish with your bare hands. We can go swimming and he can teach me. My Tia came out of the back kitchen door, her hands drying a wet casserole dish. "Don't you think you should see your grandmother first before you go running off?" David grabbed me by the arm and said "I'll show him."

Grandma had the calmest room in the house. It was dark, with fans blowing from every corner, a sweet aroma of rose water mixed with mentholated ointment. The rest of the house sweltered. A small TV flickered a Mexican soap opera while my grandmother sat on the edge of her bed. She smiled from the craziness; a fat man in a multi-colored polka dot shirt talked loudly, his voice changing octaves every sentence. Her *panza* giggled as she laughed, repeating the words the man said. "*Mijo*, come here," she said. I let her rock me in her arms, my hands pressed to the side, the cold wrinkles of her face against my eye. There wasn't much I could say. She spoke only Spanish and I was taught only English. She took my hands up, looked at the insides of my wrists and then led me to another part of her room. On a table stood a plaster statue of Mary, pictures of the Virgin Guadalupe and Saul pasted to "Eternalux" candles. There were pictures of David and me in small brass frames, a porcelain manger with baby Jesus between us. Behind our pictures was an old postcard photograph of my grandfather, long dead, his wife curled in his arms. Not so much a demand, but almost a plea, she said, "You will come back and pray? David and you?"

"Sure, Grandma, whenever." David shook his head

and told Grandma we were going to the lake. She smiled and nodded, placed her hand on David's cheek. She took a green Tupperware bowl from the nightstand, pulled a chunk of dough and started kneading tortillas, getting lost again in her soap opera, her hands becoming powdery.

It was too hot to play outside most afternoons; the temperature reached a hundred and ten. That's when grandma would pull us in her room and we'd pray for an hour or more, until we did a whole rosary. A single candle would flicker, curtains closed, black beads turned over in our hands. The silence seemed to create more space, the small room swelled to a cathedral, inducing awe and delirium in me. During prayers, I thought I could feel Jesus in my heart, the blood speeding through my arms, the belief that my actions would lead to heaven. The fan's air oscillated past my back, sending shivers through my body. Then the fan's blades turned on David. His sweat filled my nostrils. The heat and the odor made me warm and somehow I wanted to move closer to David, to inhale deeply next to him, to place my head against his shoulder, to rub my nose in his armpit. When we were done, Grandma lay down on the crochet-covered bed, her hands over her stomach as if she were out of air. My tia flicked her cleaning rag at David and me to get us outside. She'd looked in on Grandma to see if she was all right and if she left the candle burning. "You'll thank her later in your life for this," my aunt told us, as I followed David out the back door, letting it slam like he did. As my uncle said, I was David's little shadow.

David had secrets, secrets he never told anyone but me: the newspapers he set on fire in the bathtub, then stepped in; the space below his knees where he'd dig with his dinner fork until the pain felt too good. The first night in the farmhouse where David and I would sleep, he pulled up the carpet and underneath were old magazines filled with black and white photos of men and women nude on the beach. I pretended to be studious of the women's figures, pointing out their breasts. What intrigued me were the men, the abundance of hair around their dicks and asses, how many different shapes they came in, the strange musty odor off the pages themselves. I wanted to hold their crotches to my nose, let my tongue taste the magazines. Then David asked, "Do you have a boner?"

I had no idea what he was saying, like it was a word my grandmother had taught him, that it was part of some ritual. I did feel different, extremely flush, the same buoyancy inside as if I were held underwater, a similar dizziness to losing blood. Then David grabbed my dick. It made me jump, and I noticed how it swelled and felt good having him hold it, having him bend it and explain that this was a boner. I wasn't sure if I should, but he let me lightly touch his dick too, let me outline the shape, then squeeze.

As we passed the farm house, our usual destination

after prayers with grandma, David asked if I wanted to see something special. He said I couldn't tell anybody about this either. He walked quickly, deliberately, to the old barn on my uncle's lot. The door was locked but we could pull the bottom corner out and slip through the crack. It was dark inside. The smell of gasoline and hay made me nauseous. I thought he was going to show me some more dirty pictures and I started to get hard. We walked over to a workbench where there were flower pots and hand tools. There was just enough light streaming from the ceiling, punctured with holes. From the highest shelf he pulled down some red clay pots. He said, "Shh, you can't tell anyone or they'll make me bury them." I still held a smile, my dick pressed against my zipper. He brought the first pot low enough for me to look in. "Go ahead, take one out." I wasn't sure what was inside, they were small and white. When I paused, David said "They won't hurt you." As I placed my hand inside, I touched something dry and porous. I wanted to pull my hand out, but David pushed on my back. My fingers found holes to slip into, so I pulled it out quickly. Even then I wasn't sure what it was. I turned it over in a crevice of light. The shape was unintelligible, but as I looked closer teeth smiled back at me and I dropped it, the fine dirt floor absorbing the impact. David giggled, "They're mouse heads. I find them in the fields all the time. And over here are some birds." I wrinkled my nose, not sure if he shouldn't bury them. I almost didn't want to see the pot with the bird heads. Holding the pot to the light, I could make out small bluish lumps; a horrible smell came up. I could see small feathers still attached, a bit of rotted eyes, whereas the mouse skulls were sun bleached. David said over and over, "Aren't they cool? Aren't they cool?" He put his arm across my back, "But this is the best." He pulled down the last pot, "Go ahead and grab one." I did, slowly felt my way around the edge of the pot, till I felt something like very dry-textured skin. I moaned, my stomach felt sick. It was shaped like a cone or a shell. As I pulled it to the light again I couldn't make it out. It sounded as if there were tiny beads inside the shell. I shook it a little harder and asked what is it. "It's a rattler tail. Cool, huh?"

I was a little incredulous, "Oh right, come on, what is it?" I was sure it was going to be something disgusting.

"No really, it is, I'll show you." On the other side of the barn, snake skins were pinned to the old boards of the barn; he had several up, each at least a yard long.

"Yuck, did you find them dead, too?" I asked.

"No, I kill them. I go walking down the old dirt road, past the tracks. I always find them near an edge of grass. I just use rocks. I try to hit them below their heads first. I like it when their bodies squirm." I ran my finger down one of the skins, the texture feeling much drier than I imagined. David smiled, a smile I usually liked to see, a smile that meant he had pride in me, that he taught me something. He said, "The guys at the cannery buy the skins off me, they put them on their hats, but I'm going to give you one before you have to leave."

David started to put the pots back up on the shelf, almost as sacred as my grandmother's table of religious statues and family photographs. As David put the last pot up, the old shelf started to tilt, small nails came out of the wood brackets and all the pots came crashing down. Skulls fell everywhere, rattles seemed crushed under planks of wood and other pots. My tia heard the noise and came running out through the kitchen. "You boys, are you in there?" David and I looked at each other, afraid to answer. "So help me God, you better answer."

David said, "Yes, Mom."

"What are you kids up to, and what made that noise?" She tried to peek through the crack in the door, but couldn't see clearly. David and I tried to kick the skulls under the workbench, my white tennis shoes turning brown. "Get out here," my aunt yelled.

David said under his breath, "Oh Jesus, oh Jesus." I left the barn first, scraping my arm against the cracked wood, lodging a small splinter.

"God blessed, am I going to have to go get the key from the house? I want to know what happened, I want to know now!" David slipped out, holding two broken shards of my tia's pots. "Oh God, what happened?" David started to try to explain, his words jumbled and mixed up. "I guess you want your cousin to see you cry," my tia said to David. David whimpered, shaking his head. "Give me your belt, and don't give me any of your lip, boy." David stared at the ground, slowly slipping off his belt. He handed the leather weaved belt to her; she grabbed it quickly. "Bend over," she screamed. "You should be embarrassed that your cousin is going to see you cry." I was afraid, too, and stood stiffly by him. David pulled down his pants, exposing just his cheeks. When he finally stood absolutely still, she swung the belt hard. Each hit made David cry more distinctly, until his entire body crumpled onto the ground, his hands brought to his mouth, his knees pressed to his stomach. "Now pick this mess up," my aunt scowled. My grandma came outside, wanting to know what was going on. My tia gave her a look like they'd discussed something before, then walked back in the house. I tried to follow David into the barn, holding the corner of the door open. Grandma reached for my arm, wanting me to come into her room, saying it was best for David to clean up the mess himself.

"Grandma is doing another novena for you," I said. David and I were stripped to our white briefs and ready for bed, the night had not yet cooled down. David had been quiet for the whole day. Tearful from being belted, he didn't look me in the eye, tears along the edges of his eyelids, even after he'd cleaned up the mess and walked into grandma's room to join me. I pulled up the carpet in the farm house, our normal routine. I would read what I could to David, who was looking over my shoulder, trying to understand. David looked mad tonight. Above his head the moon was shaped like a nail clipping. I slept badly near the stash of porno magazines and the open window.

"I don't think you should look at those magazines," he said.

"Why not?" I asked.

"Because I'm going to tell."

"They're your magazines." David looked down on his hands, studying their shape, their strength. He then got up on his knees, then his haunches. I looked up at him, not sure what he was going to do. He then pounced on me, striking my face with a good slap, placing all his weight on top of me like a "dog pile" at school, where everyone jumps on top of one another and the bottom guy is crushed. I started to cry, afraid he was going to beat me up. I told him I was going to snitch on him, tell my uncle what he showed me. David just lay on top of me, not moving, his weight nearly crushing me. I knew I wouldn't really tell, somehow I wanted him to go farther, do something more to me, and I wondered if David knew what I wanted. I began to get hard, my body getting used to his body's weight, he then rolled off. He turned the light off and crawled into his sleeping bag. The windows sparkled with stars. I knew he had closed his eyes.

I was a light sleeper, would wake from any sound. From cracked eyes I could see David getting out of bed;

it must have been near past midnight now. Standing at a window, I could make out David's hands behind his back. He turned to look at me. I got up quietly, so as not to make the floors creak. David's body was outlined by moonlight and the fine tracing of body hair. When I stood by him, he moved over slightly to let me look outside too. At home the street lights would allow only a few stars to show. Here you could see the stretch of the Milky Way. It made me feel small, made me want to hold onto David these last few days. There was a smile on David's lips as he put his arm around my waist, as he pulled me close.

With hand signals, David got me to put my socks and hiking boots on. I whispered, "Why?" and felt unsure. He held his palm over my mouth. We both sneaked outside, careful not to make too much noise with the door. It felt good to be outside, almost naked, the night's cool temperature finally present, the strange smell of cows, dry grass, the feeling of insects grazing on my skin, chest, legs, the back of my neck. I crossed my arms over my chest, not sure someone couldn't see. David motioned me to the fields, the other side of my uncle's fence. The neighbors grew strawberries and David climbed over. I stepped on the sturdy 2x4 rung, but David insisted on helping me over. "Watch for nails," he said, his hand holding mine. When I was over he said, "Walk ahead." I led, walking in a furrow, afraid of snakes, and that my aunt and uncle would look out their window and see us. In the middle of the field

David said, "Lie down."

"Where?" As I turned around, David had stepped over to the other furrow and had lain down in it. On his chest were strawberries that he was plucking from plants nearby. "Lie down!" I did it this time, uneasy at first. The back of my calves, and my shoulders felt the unfamiliar touch of soil. I, too, started picking strawberries, slowly placing them on my chest, wondering what this was all about. I took a bite of one, it didn't taste ripe. I held it up to the moon, but could barely see even with the sky nearly white in pinpoints. David said, "Now crush them on your body." I looked over and he was covered already. He had smashed them on his face, over his crotch, and was smearing the waste over his mouth, across his forehead.

It felt stupid at first, the seedy skin breaking, the aroma of strawberries blanketing me. "Inside your underwear, too," came David's voice. I watched as he put some down his shorts, his face turned to the sky. I put one strawberry inside, pressing it down with my hand, the skin breaking near my dick. He stepped over from his furrow and offered me a hand up. His white underwear looked as if he were bleeding. Small skins fell off his stomach and his arms, leaving discolored patches on his flesh, dark and unnatural. His face was nearly shadowed; my uncle's farm was behind him. He held onto my hand and reached for my other, pulled me in an embrace. David had a pleasant odor. With my nose buried between his arm and chest, he started to rub his body against mine and I helped, sliding the juice between us, his laughter reassuring me. He stepped back and looked me over, saw the extent of our handiwork. "Now we're brothers," he said.

Hand in hand, we went further up the furrows till we came to the highway. We stood there red-stained, our hair uncombed, our underwear blood red and dirt brown. Cars would drive by and honk. No one would stop. A driver in a big rig dropped his hairy jaw as if that were all he could do. David and I looked both ways down the highway, running across the road then into the weeds. My cousin spoke softly, softer than he had ever spoken to me before: "Be careful, there might be snakes this time." The weeds grew high until we hit rocks again, a small rise in the open field, then tracks. "The train should be coming soon."

It started to get cold, I felt an urge to leave, to go back inside and wipe the strawberry marks off me. My grandma had warned me never to go near the tracks with David. David said, "Please wait, I can see the front light of the train not far away."

As the train came close David said, "Close your eyes." When I did, he made me move closer to the tracks, my body stiff and almost unwilling. He told me not to move an inch either way. I could hear the metal wheels on the metal tracks, I opened my eyes. David covered my eyes, said, "Trust me, please." When I stood absolutely still like he wanted, his hands came off me, lifted off the back of my arms. Somehow I felt comforted, as if invisible threads linked us. From across the tracks he yelled, "When it's over look over here." I could barely hear the end of the sentence. With that, all I could hear was the noise of the train, the honking of a horn, the rush of wind the train made across my body, across the field, kicking up dirt, pushing out exhaust. I thought I would fall forward, I could feel the near miss of the train, maybe inches away, an occasional light piercing my closed eyelids. The screech, whoosh, the banging of track seemed to take forever before I could open my eyes again, until the last car went by with a final perishing gust. I looked across the tracks. I didn't see David. I turned all the way around, the train now far down the track leading to Delano. I was alone and I looked back at the farm, wondering what I should do, if I should go to Grandma's room and tell her. At that moment David popped up behind the tall weeds, laughing and saying, "I told you to trust me, I told you." I stood perfectly still, unable to speak or breathe. I knew I wouldn't until he said so, my body glistening in sweat under the moon light.

Without David telling me to be silent, I held my words as we walked in the small wooden building to the far end of my uncle's lot. Along the wall I could see a sink and hose, a large tin bucket leaning on a cabinet, a bare bulb hung above. As I stepped in the wash basin, I remembered how a boy my own age I hadn't known had pulled me out of the lake as I was choking up water, his hands pressing rhythmically against my stomach, his eyes full of intent on saving my life. My grandma stood behind this boy, her hands folded, saying Hail Marys, tears running down her face to the ground. Now David pressed his hand against my chest. His touch seemed to burn somewhere deep inside me, the warmth quickly extinguished by the cool water. Strawberry skins filled the drain. I watched David's hands work, how they rubbed over the front of my body, how sturdy his wrists appeared, their strength. And still I knew where weakness ran. I looked at my own wrists, then David's. I noticed the patterns of veins stretched up his arms, they flexed as he washed me, lifting the elastic band of my briefs, spraying gently inside. He was just as thorough drying me off, with old cloth towels, stiff and musty, smelling of car wax and window cleaner. A cool breeze, like a fan, passed over us. I wanted to rush David, as if I was called for a mission, to say, "Now it is my turn, let me do you."

MY AZTLAN: WHITE PLACE

I am stinking drunk, driving down the wrong freeway back to my place. My eyes, which are getting bad, now blur even the large green exit signs, reflective dots that spell City Terrace Drive. Hours in Rage, Revolver, Motherlode and Mickey's have made me wish for my childhood home. I don't know why I'm attracted to those West Hollywood bar types — blond hair, blue eyes — who twist my gold chain with a wedding ring on it. Their fingers are pale compared to my darker skin. They run them down my neck, under my lapel. They ask where I'm from, disappointed at my answer, as if *they* are the natives.

Driving the San Bernadino is the closest I get to Mecca. I was born below this freeway, in a house with a picket fence now plowed under. It was the same street my uncle and tia lived on. I shut off the radio, quietly pass the church, a pharmacy, a corner gas station where Dad pumped tanks full of ethyl while I collected two of every animal for an ark, my free gift.

These high-power street lamps can't burn out the gang-infested walls. Black spray paint letters fuse into unlit alleys. Parked cars are tombstones. The air is sewer-scented. I've been here before, time after time, told my mother where our old house would be buried, near the call box, under the fast lane. She knows when I ramble it's the virus. She questions me about what my doctor has said, ignores my response when I say, I'm just lonely. She doesn't want to think about the white man who infected me. "He might as well have shot you," she said once. My mother let me know that she turns in her sleep, sick at the thought of his dick up my ass or in my mouth. A milky white fluid floats in my body's space, breaks into the secret bonding of her sex, my father's sex, and the marriage of their cells.

I unleash the seat belt, stare at the ivy embankment. A brick wall hides the flow of cars, the veins and arteries of downtown. I am more conscious of my heart, can sense the pressure as my fingers grasp the locked steering wheel. I am not afraid of getting shot, a stray bullet to the head. I've been through worse, can take whatever this "Dog City" as the news portrays it can dish out. I would welcome a quick end. I have watched my lover and friends melt away, their hands held in mine. The last of their body's heat: fuel to move me along, to my own impending death.

I imagine the house still intact, buried under dirt and asphalt, dust and neglect. Hidden under a modern city, this is my Aztlan, a glimpse of my ancient home, my family. All it takes is a well-chosen phrase to cave in: Mom, why did you burn my hands with the iron and say it was an accident? tattoo my arms with the car's cigarette lighter? make me wish your wish, that I was never born? make me admit they are all lies? I starved and you refused your breast, lavished me instead with gifts and I would destroy them, pile them in a corner, dolls without eyes, legs, heads. Like the house, these words spiral in on themselves, stab into the moist earth and rot; the angry lords eat their own. Ivy grows over this hell hole. The sprinklers kick on. The traffic roars.

Back at my apartment, I rifle through a six-pack, turn on the set, feel like I've been in a hit-and-run accident, so I pick the windshield glass out of my skin. My father would get this drunk, call me out of my bed to hold me. I would be hot in flannel bed clothes, but I wouldn't struggle. He held me like a rag doll, my face in his warm armpit, my waist wrapped in his legs. He would kiss my scalp, call me *mijo*. His brown mechanic's hand would slip under my shirt, rub my stomach. He'd press his finger in the hole, my umbilical cord's scar till I screamed, writhing and laughing. My mother hated my father like this. When he wasn't drunk, he was gone, back at the plant or the Garfield Lanes. She would yank me by the arm away from him. He'd hold me tighter between his thighs, my free arm around his neck because I wanted to stay. My arm would get sore; she would give up; he would pet me till we both fell asleep, his breath the only air I breathed.

My lover never understood why I hated to be tickled, why I liked to be tied up. AIDS killed him before I could say a word, my past stored under a heavy lid, burnished pottery. When he was alive, he made it easy to leave my folks behind. I became white, too, uncolored by age in his over-forty crowd. For our sake, I kept Sleepy Lagoon, Indian massacres, and insecticides taboo subjects to avoid arguments and misunderstandings. My lover played no part in these atrocities. I believed that the color of our skin didn't matter, there was only he and I in this affair. He offered his life and I ate greedily. Like a disease-ridden blanket, revenge was on my parents, to be gay and not speak Spanish.

I run to the toilet to puke, a steady stream pours out of my mouth. An empty AZT shell comes, then foam. It floats on the water's tension, circles the bowl and disappears. It has become ritual to lie on the cold tile, stare at the mold patched ceiling, skip another set of pills, what some people call hope. My stomach cramps so I strip. I can smell the sweat off my shirt, my jeans stick to my legs. My street sleeps. All I can hear is water splash against porcelain. It sprays down my throat and tongue, flushes out the sides. I taste the metal in the pipes. This is my love, late night showers, to scrub my skin with a stiff washcloth and glycerine soap. When I was a kid, I used to think Mexicans were greasy because of the foods they ate, heavy in lard. My mother served fried beans and fried hamburger all the time. Later, I would wash as if to peel skin, to leave nothing but dry flesh, to get the oil out.

My hair is still wet when I get under the bed sheet. I am alone again. My head clears and throbs against the damp pillow, faint car lights run across the walls. I haven't been this fucked up in a long time, not since my lover threatened to leave. I had put a row of beer cans with pull tabs on the coffee table. I drank one after another till he noticed. I was crying because we hadn't had sex in a month, because he couldn't get hard, because he didn't love me anymore: my suspicion. I kept on drinking four, five, six, crushing cans just like Dad. He protested, "This isn't fair, stop playing games." But it was no game, this was the best I felt in a long time, this was the only pleasure I was going to get that night. I tried to crawl back to his body, after, to sleep in his arms. He turned away. A month passed and he died. The virus had gotten into his brain. It had made its first appearance as exhaustion, then shingles, thrush and meningitis. He didn't know me at the end. His face was just as unfamiliar, forty pounds thinner, bones and colors I didn't recognize. His last words: "When are you going to grow up?"

I want to feel better, so I grab a little lube, think back farther, when I was young, went to parties in the hills with my lover's friends and his former lovers. They all treated me as a son, this little Mexican boy. They'd say, "You're not like the rest." I was newly acquainted with the doctor's condo, the lawyer's palace, high above the valleys. They shoveled coke, double hit poppers or smoked Tai; they would let me rest, small, unintimidated, in the folds of their leather, they would rub my nose in their heat. They said stuff like, "Hot latin, brown-skinned, warm, exotic, dark, dark, dark," buried under their bodies' weight, dirt and asphalt, moist skin, muscle and blood. My face collides with their chests, their hearts are at my eardrums, their fire cracks louder than guns.

I beat off to their memories, dust and neglect, the pressure of their thighs, the crush against my mouth. My belief, when my skin has been oiled up, is that I won't be in so much pain afterwards. There is no punishment. I will come home. I can feel my body becoming tar, limbs divide, north and south. My house smells of earth and it rumbles from the traffic above. White clay sifts through the ceiling. My bones shine in the dark.

UNPROTECTED

I cannot get this smell of hand lotion off of me. I've washed three times today, covered myself in cologne, sat in the steam room so that I could sweat it all out; but it's still there. It is faint in my beard. It is underneath my nails and I can smell it when I bring food to my mouth. It is here in my bed. It smells of cock and ass. It smells unnatural. It smells unsafe.

I knew I was too drunk, six bars already that afternoon, and on the Sunday that I promised my parents I would visit them. They wanted to have dinner with me, watch some TV. They worried about my ARC diagnosis, but they would never ask about it. They wondered when was I going to look like those men they had seen on the news, men who were dying of AIDS. They wanted to know when was I going to be sorry for the things that I did to get this way.

AIDS had already become an issue when I came out in '83. I was twenty-one. So along with the usual guilt trips to stop me from coming out: "What will your father say?" "What will your brothers say?" "Where did I go wrong?" my mother asked, "Aren't you afraid?"

"But, Mom, I'm in love." He was ten years older, wiser, blond hair, blue eyes, a furry chest. I loved the way he'd grab my ass, would tell me, "Come on, baby, let me fuck you."

It wasn't a tragedy to move out, but I could hear my father crying, hitting the drywall that separated his room from mine. My mother sat at the dining room table, with its lion claw feet tearing into her slippers. She just stared into the china cabinet and wept.

John had met me at his door. He told me I could live with him forever. I lived with him for more than four years, then he died. I don't know why he ever went out with me. I couldn't even imagine going out with a kid of twenty-one. I tested soon after his death. A friend had said, "Not even cold in the grave yet." I found out that I only had thirty-five T-cells, my platelet count was critical, and I needed a transfusion. Since then, I've stabilized, I have no symptoms except low T counts. I rarely think about being sick when I take my AZT capsules.

On this day, I took my four o'clock pills with a swig of beer and headed for a new bar. My friend Nick drove. We'd been friends for more than ten years, since elementary school. It was this last bar that did me in. It was called The Brick. It had a rougher edge than the rest of the west-end bars. Today it proudly proclaimed it was "Hawaiian Daze," stenciled in black marker over a cheap Tom of Finland poster. It showed two sailors; one had his hand down the other's pants.

Nick and I were feeling great; our feet dragged in the white sand that was thrown on the hardwood floor. A cut-out hula dancer was pinned at her nipples to a cork bulletin board, and the moose head was strangled by a thin red lei. As we walked further into the bar, two men in leather jackets, faces uncut by razors, hair cropped to the skin, sporting grass skirts and fishnet stockings, lay on the pool table. They waved under the blow-up shark that was spinning like a record. Everyone was flashing back to disco, The Village People and their hits, "YMCA" and "Macho Macho Man." They showed one of the singers on the video monitor, a telephone lineman, working the pole, his jeans ripped just below the crotch. Everyone was screaming and I was full of their energy. I was ready to explode. I needed to do something, make something happen, and like a cat, I pawed at the great white shark, suspended by the smallest test line. It made the bar stir, its waters already in a frenzy.

Nick and I played pool in the back room, smoking

cigarettes and drinking vodka tonics. I was losing badly, knocking the striped balls into a pocket, making the cue jump in the air and land a few inches away. Missing shot after shot, I gave up. I put my head down on the table, in line of Nick's victory and told him, "Shoot the fucking ball, I'm ready." That's when I saw him.

His handlebars caught my eye, making me turn my head. Nick was still at the table trying some impossible trick. I bounced the rubber tip of the pole between my legs, grinning. This guy looked straight at me. I didn't really expect him to sit down next to me, on my stack of beer crates. I didn't think I was attractive enough, especially now with the virus. He wore a pink madras shirt buttoned down to his stomach; his confidence was apparent. His rib cage was strong and voluminous. There was a serpentine chain around his throat. It clung tightly and moved when he said, "Do you want to go to my place?"

John had always said it was that easy. Go up to a guy and ask him point blank. I had thought it was a bit sleazy. I imagined it should be more like a wild bird ritual, with ruffled feathers, heavy squawking, and beaks intermingled. I really had no experience cruising, it seemed to have become some lost art form. I thought about it, saying, "Well, maybe. What's your name?" The music was too loud and I just winged it, catching his question again, "Do you want to go to my place?" Nick was setting up another game. I told him, tugging on a loop on his jeans, "I'll see you later." I staggered out of the bar, following a man whose name I didn't hear.

We stopped at Rocky's liquor on the way to his place. I asked for a Pepsi. He came back with Coronas and a pot of spider mums. Driving up to the hills, he told me they were for a friend who was sick in the hospital. He started talking about his condo, saying it was real nice. He then told me he had brought someone up there once and was ripped off. He talked philosophically of Louise Hay. He told me of his gay brother who lived across the street, pointing out the top floor of a refurbished hotel. It had a history. Hollywood's best actresses had all lived there at one time. He started reciting the prices of other condos around his. I put my hand on his lap.

Inside the garage, we walked side by side. His steps were hard, his businesslike shoes hit cement covered with water. The puddles reflected the bars of fluorescent light. They shook nervously as we went by, while the chrome doors of the elevator opened for us. He held the door open for me with his arm. When I stepped in, he pressed the stop button. I thought that maybe he wanted to kiss me or something. Instead he looked at me, as if he wanted me to stare down. I did, embarrassed at what I was doing. He asked if I was a hustler. I said no. He didn't seem convinced.

He wasn't going to touch me, even after I crossed the threshold. Without much grandeur, he showed each of his rooms. The place was beautiful. There were beveled glass tables and shelves, a leather sectional. Each room was immaculate, unlike my place. There were dishes in my sink that I would sooner throw out than wash. He led me to his balcony. Comfortable chairs of azure were accented by a pale blue rattan table, on which thick green candles absent of burning wicks rested. He unbuckled his pants, then sat down, rubbing his cock, thumbing the shaft. He then pulled out his balls, letting them rest over the teeth of his zipper.

Other apartments crowded in on us, like a cubist painting. The large black windows were opaque because of the screen that was made not to be seen through. There was no space here either, no breathing room. I thought that other people could see us out here with his fly open. I undid my belt and pulled on my button jeans. I told him I like the sound of Levi's opening.

He got up to get us a drink. He said from the kitchen, "Did you notice I have no curtains." Coming back out on the balcony he said, "I have nothing to hide." I looked around: there were no curtains, no blinds. "Just doors," I thought.

I had to hide everything. Like the gold wedding band that is on a chain my parents had given me. The chain has a cross on it, too. I had promised my parents that I'd wear the cross all the time. They didn't know I wore it with John's ring. To them it would seem immoral; John got me sick. Clothes can hide these defects, like the blue-red pinpoints on my veins, a sign of bimonthly blood workups and the virus. I wonder if he could tell, if that's why his smile was a bit wicked. I thought at this point I should be responsible and make sure we play safe. I didn't want to get too carried away.

He started walking toward me, to the bedroom that was behind me. I stopped him, "I'm feeling a little uncomfortable, maybe we should talk first."

He said gently and reassuringly, "Don't worry, I won't hurt you." The words fell out of him like a whisper. I did begin to worry. First he tells me about getting ripped off by some previous trick, he asks me if I was a hustler, now he tells me don't worry I won't hurt you.

I said, "I should tell you something first." I hesitated, afraid of rejection, as his face changed to annoyance. I went on, "I'm positive." I felt like a child confessing his sins, kneeling in a dark room. I felt or thought that maybe he was positive, too. He talked about his sick friend, the Hay group, it seemed probable that he had the virus.

His face registered nothing. "I tested negative to HIV." It hit me like a broom. I saw him in my imagination, in the tearooms getting blown near the porcelain bowls, cruising parks under lattice-covered walkways, walking around in a wet white towel at a bathhouse late at night. I knew I was being unfair to him, thinking that he was some seedy person who escaped the curse. I saw him do these things, in my mind, things that are considered unsafe, almost sinful now. I couldn't help but feel cheated, I had done none of these things. I didn't deserve this disease.

He sat back in his chair, lighting a cigarette. "Do you feel comfortable with this?"

I said, "I feel a little weird."

"Like how?"

"Like I'm infectious material." He winced at this remark. I saw myself being transported in an orange-red garbage bag, getting tossed out by sallow-colored gloves.

Recomposed, he said rather smugly, almost challenging me, "Well, if you don't feel right about this, it's fine with me. I accept myself for what I am." I thought it must be easy when you're negative. With a softer voice he said, "We can just beat off." I took a drink from my beer. Cold liquid went inside of me, shutting down parts of me like a machine. He closed his argument. "That's all we have to do." He pulled off his shirt and hung it over the rail. I began to undress in the doorway of his bedroom.

He uncovered his bed neatly, folding the spread in half, then quarter. His room was spotless. Lights came from behind the head-board. The cream-colored wood twisted like a Bernini pulpit. The shadows bent around the corners of the room. The ceiling sparkled with glitter. One wall was all closet doors. He opened one, placing the comforter on the center shelf. I expected him to pull out a plain percale to protect his Southwestern sheets. Sheets like that need to stay clean and sex was dirty. He just pulled down his pants. I took my lead from his, tossing my shirt to the floor, lacking his grace for folding.

We got on the bed slowly, our knees pressing into the soft mattress. He reached for my left nipple and I withdrew. His hands were cold as the air coming through the open door. He stuck his fingers into my mouth to warm them. I felt their tips on my jagged back teeth. My tongue tasted the saline skin pulling out, over my lips, then slipping back in again. I was like a scavenger, hands tearing the hair that grew over his shoulders, tugging at his prick, pointed upright and bent. I was gentle with his foreskin, letting it peel back on its own; but he asked for more, "Pull harder, grip it tighter, twist it around." He reached behind me for the nightstand and brought out a bottle of hand lotion. He poured it on the both of us. The cool, motherly scent filled the room and oppressed me. I couldn't get hard now. When he made me hold out my hand, I couldn't help but think of my mother using this every day. She would put it on, spreading it evenly over her arms and white hands. She would remove her wedding ring that clutched a diamond. I also remembered mornings when John would pour it on his shoulders and ask me to rub it in. He would fall on the bed and wait for me. After I finished, I would cuddle into his side, trying to stay warm, drifting back into dreams.

I kept on shrinking, becoming smaller and smaller. I thought of how I hated hand cream as a lubricant. I said, disappointed, "Go ahead and finish, I can't."

He stopped stroking his cock and looked at mine,

limp and unexcited. He asked me, "Why don't you spend the night?" Then without any response from me, he pulled me under his covers, wrapping his legs over my body. His thighs became binding material. I could hear him mumble something. I started trying to fall asleep, glad because of all the alcohol that was inside me, making the room spin. His hard dick was still touching me, coming up inside the crack of my ass. He wasn't sleeping. His mouth was at the back of my neck, warm air blowing on my nape. I stared out the open glass door that led to the balcony, where this whole thing started. I thought that maybe I shouldn't have said anything about being positive, that if I could get his leg off me, I could get up and put my clothes back on and leave.

He was so near, he whispered, "Why don't you lie on your back?" He got to his knees and I could see the shadowy outline of him against the shimmering ceiling, the textured surface embedded with glitter. Shadows were thrown onto every wall and corner, lewd shapes of worms, snakes and mushrooms. His chest billowed like a sail. I became his cabin boy, learning the ropes. My ankles began to sweat. My wrists were held down by the weight of his hands and body. He sat on my chest and I could smell his cock a few inches from my face, taunting me. He told me, "Suck that dick," and I did. I didn't even hesitate. I swallowed him like meat. It made me choke. "You like that big dick, don't you?" I nodded. It seemed enormous, really too big. I began to split in half.

One side of me was screaming, "This is wrong. This is unsafe. What are you doing?"

The other side said, "Shut up, you're going to die anyway. Enjoy this because this is going to be your last time."

It was easy to take him in. My mouth stretched as wide as it could. My chin would rub against his balls, regulating his speed. The hair on my face would mix with the hair on his nuts, and they would pull on each other. He began to pump hard and I gagged. Later, his hands were between my legs, his fingers touching my ass. I knew I would let him fuck me, there wasn't even an afterthought.

I couldn't sleep in the unfamiliar room, quiet now as a church. At five in the morning I picked up my things, the damp shirt, my wrinkled jeans, my unlaced shoes. I ran to catch the bus and it waited for me. It was filled with Mexicanos, some from South America. The men all looked at me as I entered, and I took my seat quickly. I was afraid they could smell the shit that was in my beard, see the sticky shine of cum over my body, and know what I had done that night. Each one of those short, stocky men with their black hair and Indian profiles would know. The seat next to me was empty until a young Mexican man sat down. He spread his legs open till they touched mine. The bus tore down the street, hitting a pothole. It jarred the riders and made my neighbor rub his leg against mine. He smiled at me.

I pulled my legs together, closing them tight. I fell asleep against the window that was cracked open, my hands acting as a pillow, breathing in the exhaust from outside and the lotion that was over my hands, heavy as spring air.

HOLY

Next door in my apartment building lives a woman who doesn't bathe. I had noticed her the first day I moved in; the hallway was pungent with her odor. I can see her from my rear window, running out the back door, garbage in her hands. She quickly disposes of the material as if she's embarrassed. She wears bright red lipstick, no other makeup, and the same stained, yellow jumpsuit day after day, the cuffs and hems blackened. Her hair is always wet.

She stays home every day, like me; she obviously doesn't work. When my taxi pulled up, I saw her staring out the lobby window. I felt odd, her watching what I was doing. Since I didn't have to pay the driver — a service for the disabled — I felt feeble walking behind the driver, carrying my free groceries from the food bank. That night, with the heavy rains keeping us in, I could hear her through our connecting kitchen wall, speaking to herself, slamming cabinet doors, banging pots. I tried placing a glass against the wall. I couldn't make out any of her words, so I turned the radio on, a little louder than it had to be. The next morning, I was walking past her door and she opened it. In her living room I noticed moving-boxes everywhere, some without lids. In that split second passing her door, I could tell she had no money to speak of, no furniture, that she lived minimally. She slammed her door when she saw it was me. I ran down the hallway and threw the front door open. I had a doctor's appointment and couldn't be late.

When I arrived home, there were cards of saints and martyrs taped haphazardly on my front door. One woman was sinking in a lake, another woman's eyeballs were on a silver platter. I pulled the cards off the door, thought they might have been from one of my friends, everyone knew how I really enjoyed tacky religious objects. Or it could have been the woman across the street who sold me the clock with the 3D pictures of Jesus on the Cross and at the Last Supper. She knew where I lived, and I made a note to call her later to thank her for the gifts.

That night, I had already stripped for bed, was under

the sheets, reading a journal of a Frenchman who died of a sexually transmitted disease. I could hear the woman and her usual ranting next door. For a moment it stopped and so I thought I could fall asleep. Out in the hallway, I could hear someone walking slowly, making the floorboards creak. I rolled onto my side. I could see light under the front door and the shadows of two feet in front. I waited to hear a knock. Nothing. I closed my eyes, thinking the shadows were my imagination; that's when I could hear whispering, then the sound of scotch tape being pulled from its dispenser. I got out of bed quietly, sneaked up to the peephole. When I looked outside, nothing. I could hear the door next to mine click shut. I opened my door. There was a lone white candle burning at my feet and a bowl of white rice with chopsticks; around the candle were cards with saints taped to the carpet and the corners of the door jamb. The next morning I called the apartment manager and told him what had happened, who I thought it was. He said, "She is no harm, just be patient and she'll stop." The next evening, it happened again. And still the manager refused to do anything. I started seeing her more and more on the street. I saw her from across Hollywood Blvd., at my doctor's office, in the parking lot of my pharmacist, on the back of the bus I take to the hospital where I get my x-rays done to check for pneumonia or new growths. I called the police, confessed that I had this deadly disease and didn't need this added stress, that this woman was driving me crazy.

Once I sat reading the newspaper at the patio table behind the apartment. She came and seated herself across from me. I threw the paper down and yelled, "What do you want from me?" When she wouldn't answer, I got up to leave. She stood up, too, in front of me. I walked to the side of her, but again she moved. I was getting mad, I yelled, "Get the fuck away!" I shoved her hard on the shoulders and ran inside. That night a more elaborate shrine was built in front of my door. This one consisted of chewed-up pieces of paper, saliva covering the wads, candle drippings on the door handle, chicken bones and shaving cream done in an arabesque design. I took Polaroids and gave them to the police. All they could offer was that if I pushed her again I could be arrested, or if she pushed back they could arrest her. But really she was within her rights if the manager didn't stop her. The manager wouldn't. Every day the shrine grew; when I came back from the doctor, I always expected to find some new aspect. Months ago she started doing the whole hallway, and my mailbox seemed to be a special area for cut flowers, tin cans filled with water, juice, milk and urine. The other neighbors seemed to enjoy the little surprises every day, they would stand around the lobby, solemn as if they were in a museum of holy artifacts. A trio of deaf lesbians living upstairs joined in, finding different shards of colored glass and created mosaics along the stairwell. I noticed they would walk over it barefooted, cutting their soles without care. When I would come outside, their hands would flutter and then stop completely, their faces smoothed into awe. The men in the building began to construct Santa Fe-styled shelves, in greens and bronze, while their wives placed earthen jars they bought at garage sales. They would fill them with dried flowers, herbs, sand with labels of Santa Barbara, Malibu, Pismo.

The construction had been quiet for a week, and I was going outside less and less. Unwashed, I reeked of burdock and rosemary. My complexion changed from metallic gold to a deep Indian blue. I could hear whispering from every wall in my place that connected with another apartment. Now I knew how Joan of Arc felt. As I looked out my peephole, I could see that a chair, a throne had been placed there. An arc of flowers covered the chair, the shelves seemed to radiate from the chair, and all the bowls of rice, burning candles, and wads of chewed newspaper made a design at the foot of the chair. I walked out slowly into the deserted hallway. Everyone was outside, feasting on pineapple slices and wedges of guava and persimmon. I moved liked a child sneaking out of bed. I looked at the chair, then sat down. Slowly I put my head back against the cushion, gripped the padded hand rests, closed my eyes. I stopped breathing, felt when my neighbors' chants hit certain tones it filled an empty place inside me, like nourishment for my heart and liver, pulse and brain wave. In my right palm I could feel a small flame ignite and in my left, the beginning framework of a new home, the skeleton of a new being.

BAPTISM

I am always the first one up, before my cousin sleeping in the bed next to mine, or my father who never sleeps too well until a few hours before he's got to leave for work. The sun is barely visible, a glimmer of blues and reds runs along the slowly spinning blades of the ceiling fan. It is just before summer, the last day of school. Still in my nightgown, I go the mirror and brush my hair quickly. On the dresser is an old birthday card. "Happy Thirteenth Birthday!" On the card there's an Easter Bunny carrying a basket of colored eggs, on the bottom front corner written in red ink, "To my daughter Angela, Love Dad '70." My father always confuses my birthday, which is near Christmas, with my mother's birthday, which is near Easter. Last year he remembered whose birthday it was and tore the envelope and card up, threw the pieces into the trash. The pieces were stained with coffee grounds. My father cursed himself, pounding his hands into his thighs. He asked, "Why can't I get that bitch out of my head?"

After I put my hair brush down, I move quietly out of my room to make my father's coffee and fix his lunch and mine. Coming into the dining room, next to the kitchen, I look at the curio cabinet filled with photographs of the family. My father is in there in his army uniform, and I with my fourth grade class, making a face. There are other strange photographs in frames — my father holding me as a child, next to him a form cut out with scissors. There are several, like ghosts caught on film. The borders are jagged against the felt covered backs.

My father has shown me pictures of what my mother looked like before they were married — long slick black hair, the curved nose of a Mexican, lips that pressed together too tightly. My mother was everything my father wasn't: tall, arrogant and free. My father has told me parts of the story of why she left, how she fell in love with one of the neighbor boys. Other versions, soaked in tequila, say the boy was drafted, that my mother became pregnant with the soldier's baby. When he confesses this version, Dad cries dolorous tears; she loved the soldier more than her daughter and husband combined, and God paid her back by striking the soldier dead in a land-mine. When my father first told me this, I figured it must be true: there was a house that flew a flag at half-mast and had a wreath with a black ribbon on the front door in the neighborhood where we lived. Since then, I am always ashamed when I have to pass by this house.

I turn the white blinds open in the kitchen, switch the radio on, pull coffee and white bread out of the refrigerator. The news announcer finishes his report about the recent developments in the war, then turns to local news. Tonight, he reports, there will be a lunar eclipse and the weather will be extremely hot. I measure out coffee for the percolator, counting out ten rounded spoonsful. I can hear my father getting up, moaning loudly as he sits on the edge of his bed. I plug in the coffee maker quickly so it will be finished when my father comes out of the bathroom.

My cousin Denise comes into the kitchen next. She is brushing her long brown hair, one side, then the other. She pours out some orange juice for herself, makes me sit down while she brushes my hair more thoroughly. She compliments me on how blue my black hair is, how clear my face has become. I hate this kind of attention, the fussing over my complexion, the texture of my hair. Still, I let Denise treat me like a doll. It reminds me of my aunt, when Tia Roxie, my mother's sister, was alive. Denise and I would go visit her in the hospital after school. We'd spend all our time with her, brushing the thin wisps of hair on her head. I would gently massage lotion on her hands, ignore the blackened or missing nails. Roxie had lost all her sight a few years after my mother left. In the hospital room, Roxie would cry out for her sister. Denise and I would place our hands in my aunt's palm and say, "Hush, I'm here. Please try to sleep." It was Denise and I who discovered my aunt dead in the hospital, no one having checked on her for a while. She was the last of the adult women in our family; our grandmother died before Denise and I were born.

My father drags his feet coming into the kitchen while Denise finishes my hair. With both hands I lift the length of my hair, exposing the back of my neck. I tell them I want to cut my hair short. Both Dad and Denise look horrified. I let it fall down my back in one large sweep.

The classroom is hot, all the windows are leaning open and a circular fan is blowing from the teacher's desk toward the students. Miss Kroyle moves nervously, as if she wants us to tell her what a great teacher she has been this year, her first year teaching Social Studies. She positions her chair from behind her desk, near my seat. "So that nothing will block my way," she says. A small number of students have brought extra credit reports of current events to read in class. Miss Kroyle is always interested in the human factor of each report.

She sighs heaviest at what the last boy has brought, a report on the withdrawal of troops and the casualties to the villagers. She asks, "Why can't we give peace a chance?" After looking at each one of our faces staring blankly back, she continues. I smile when she comes to me. "I'm only twenty-five, not much more than a child myself, not much older than the boys fighting over there. It just doesn't make sense." She stands up, speaks more clearly: "In five years, all the boys in this class could be shipped off to the war, no choice. They'll be old enough to kill and be killed. They might not come back, and if they do they'll be scarred, wounded, arms and legs blown off." Miss Kroyle begins to cry and turns her back to the class. The students, not knowing what to do, think she means class is over and begin gathering their books and papers. They make little if any noise, as if they would wake her and it would mean more schoolwork. I quietly push my chair under the table and open the door slowly to sunlight.

When I get home, the house already seems unbearably hot. My father and I have gotten into the habit of barbecuing outdoors every night. Denise marinates the steak and chicken while I wrap the corn, mushrooms and cherry tomatoes in aluminum. My uncle will come over only after my father has arrived. Dad changes into his cut-off jeans and green rubber thongs. He unbuttons his shirt and lets his fat belly roll over his belt. I love the look of my father's chest, the dark wiry hair that grows only on his breastbone and around his nipples. He smells of his musk deodorant. Denise is always quiet when her father comes around. Dad tries to get them to speak, to tell them jokes. He starts the joke with Denise and gives my uncle the punchline. Denise smiles sullenly, walks away to the fire or the kitchen, her head held downward. My uncle's eyes look like bullets of blood.

Denise's own eyes looked in strife the day she had moved in with us. Our fathers yelled at each other loudly, my father repeating, "Your own daughter? Your own flesh?" My uncle was slurringly drunk. He bawled, "Denise, *mija,* come here. I'm sorry. I'm drunk. I didn't want to touch you. It meant nothing. I love you. Come here!" Denise stood still with her back against my bedroom door. Even with the lights turned off in my room, I could see she'd been crying. Her father cried out over my own father's voice, "I demand you come here or I wash my hands of you." Denise wouldn't move from the door, her hands around her throat like she'd been choked, or she was trying to hug herself, to give herself comfort. On my bed, I was thinking she must have been caught sneaking out at night, popping out the window screen of her bedroom. I've caught her many times, and all she did was shush me. I've heard the car that drives by slowly to pick her up. I've seen her with her boyfriend, a dark-eyed boy, eighteen or nineteen, and she was just sixteen.

My eyes were full of accusations. Denise and I stared

at each other. I turned on the small student lamp near my bed. Tears were like blood on her face and for a moment I wanted to taste each tear, swallow it up inside me. Denise tried to explain, her hands seeming to want to mold the words in front of her. On her shoulder was a duffel bag — shirts and jeans hung out the end. Her father howled, "You can keep her, God damn it!" Denise showed me how her father's beard had scratched her cheeks. I took the duffel bag and began to arrange the dresser, clearing half of my things away for her possessions, dumping the two top drawers for her, taking the larger bottom drawer for myself. I got clean white sheets from the closet and the quilt I always keep at the foot of my bed. I made her a bed, on the floor, near the window. I thought, "She should be able to breathe better there."

My father pours the last of his beer on the small grill, and smoke plumes up. He sits next to my uncle on their lawn chairs, drinking the last cold beers from the cooler. Their laps hold bones, the meat chewed off, aluminum foil crunched up into a ball. Denise and I sit on the front porch with the radio on behind us, playing songs from Motown. We press our knees together and eat slowly. We let the butter melt on the corn, the tomato seeds run into our palms, and our meat's drizzle flow into cups made of foil.

"Look! Can you see it?" These are the first words that my uncle says loudly to all of us. My uncle's finger points just above the horizon. My Dad squints, putting on the glasses he had folded into his shirt pocket. I move over to my uncle's side, try to follow the path his finger makes in the air. He says, "It must be some kind of plane, but it's too high."

"Maybe it's a satellite," I pipe up. I see why my uncle broke his silence. It is like a small star, except it is bouncing around in the sky, back and forth, up and down. Denise moves next to me while I let my father follow the path I now make with my finger. Tonight is the clearest it has been in a long time, the wind having blown all the smog away. Even the street lights don't seem to hinder the stars from becoming visible. The moon slowly makes its change from cold white to hellish red. My uncle asks me, "Do you think it's a UFO?" He points at the moving star.

My cousin answers, "No."

A few weeks after school ends, my father begins to date a woman he has met at work. She has curly black hair and smokes constantly. Denise rides with us, while my uncle follows. My father mentions this is where he used to go when he was young. He has told me privately that my mother and he often came here when they first got married. Even then, he believed, she showed signs of leaving him; it is so clear now. She was too young and only marrying him to escape her mother's home. It might not have been her fault, he said, it might not be anyone's fault.

Dad's girlfriend offers Denise a cigarette, and I can't believe that she actually takes one. She uses the lighter in the side door and opens the ashtray. She looks at me as she inhales and coughs, says my funny face makes her laugh. Dad's girlfriend offers to fix Denise's dad up with a friend of hers, if she likes. Denise takes a long drag of the cigarette, her arms crossed, she seems to stare out the window, watching the fields go by. When she exhales, she shrugs, "I don't care." Denise looks at me, and lets me sneak a hit off her cigarette.

When we arrive, Denise gets out first to look at the lake. She is happier than I have seen her in along time. She comes down the small slope doing cartwheels. My uncle can hear her laughing as he unpacks his car. He has the lawn chairs and fishing poles that he and my dad are going to use. Dad's girlfriend keeps her hands on her hips, watching everyone do something until finally my father brings her a lawn chair. She takes the chair, sits under the shade of a pine, the wind brushing the top branches, needles falling on her head. Denise and I get our beach blankets and sit by the lake. Our fathers announce that they are moving to where there is more shade because the fish are probably there. Dad's new girlfriend seems easily contented with that; she continues to read the book she has brought.

The lake is brown where we are, pine needles soaking the bottom, turning everything bronze and acidy. A little farther out the water clears to blue, and that is where we will swim. Denise pulls out bologna sandwiches on Wonder Bread, root beer and Fritos corn chips. Dad's girlfriend looks in the cooler with us and complains, "They took all the beer!"

After we finish our sandwiches, we decide to put our feet in the water. Dad's girlfriend brings out a project she's been working on. She says, "Look what I'm doing, girls." She is finishing a macrame pot holder made of azure-colored rope. She remarks she is willing to teach us, if we want. Denise replies that we are going swimming instead. Dad's girlfriend mutters, "Suit yourself."

Denise and I walk to the edge of the lake; we can see our fathers coming back, trying to show us the small fish that they caught. I notice under the sunlight that Denise's hair has lightened to a gold-brown; she smells of sweet lip gloss and baby shampoo. I know all the boys like Denise, but she turns everyone down. At school, the boys follow me, tell me what a tease Denise is, and how it is going to get her in trouble, that they had already heard stories. I wanted to whip around and hit them, come charging with my school books I was ready to throw at them. They laughed, said I was too young to say such words.

We lie back on the beach towels. I am a little higher up the bank than Denise. She moves her head near my arm, lets her hair fan out over my elbow; it commingles with my own hair. The sun seems to want to put an end to this; the heat bores into our flesh, my legs hurt. I am the first to leave, to plunge into the water, to open my eyes underneath. The water is greenish, the bottom silky with algae. It is a minute before I break for air, and as I rise, Denise jumps in. She's a much better swimmer than I am and begins to backstroke out toward the middle of the lake, her slender arms like windmills. Water trickles from her palms, runs the length of her arm in small drops and rivulets. On shore my father begins the fire, readies the meat. My uncle returns with more beer.

Denise is far out in the center of the lake and I dive underneath. The water stings my eyes but I become used to it. I stop for a moment, feel my foot tangle in some kind of line. I move back underwater to see if I can free myself and the line begins to cut. I see blood rise through the water, a bottle is under my foot and I can't free it from the line. I try to sit down, but the blood keeps coming out. I pull on the line but my hands are unable to get a good grip. I try to bite the line, and feel the air leaving my lungs. My heart seems stuck in the wrong place. A feeling begins to come over me, a warm feeling of having nothing to worry about. I let go of the string and realize that I am staring at the sun through the water of the lake, the edges of the sun changing as the waves come over me.

It feels as if I have been under the water forever, my ears are muffled, but I can make out my name being called. Above me I believe an angel is swimming by. Her hair is long and flowing, her face blocks out the sun. All at once there is a smile across her face, then something I imagine as fear. She swims down to me, and in her arms she pulls me up to air. But it feels as if I don't need air now, my ears are assaulted with yells and screams. I imagine they are reprimanding me, but Denise's voice is clear, pleading with God, telling me I can't leave her. Denise's face is close enough to kiss. As my uncle places me along the shore, tears or water fall from her lips to mine. I can see my father, arms crossed, I can read his lips, they mouth "stupid." Dad's girlfriend keeps shoving him toward me. Denise moves my face to hers, our eyes lock. Still she looks panicky and I can't understand. She places her mouth over mine and breathes into my mouth. Nothing happens. She turns me over on my stomach, pressing down into the small of my back. I feel water coming out of my mouth, running into the grass. She places my arms above my head and then I begin to feel my lungs move. I gasp and choke.

As soon as we get home, I whisper to Denise that tonight is the night. At first she doesn't get what I'm telling her. "To cut my hair." Denise shakes her head, explains she has a date, that my father would be mad. I tell her he won't even care. "What can he do after it's done." Denise holds my hair in her hand, "It's so beautiful, I don't understand how you could want to lose it." I hand her a pair of chrome scissors.

In the bathroom she gathers my hair between her hands, my head down in the sink. She murmurs that she was so afraid of losing me, that she thought I'd never breathe. The sounds of water splash against my ears and the white porcelain. Denise folds a towel around my neck and takes a section of hair. With the shears against my head, she asks, "How short do you want it?" I am thirteen, old enough to make this decision. I show her where to cut with my finger, the very top of the neck, above the ears. I can feel each section being taken off. Out of the corner of my eye, I can see Denise placing each tassel on a sheet of brown tissue paper. She cries with each cut.

When I unwrap the towel from my head, my father smiles, still a little drunk. He comes forward to kiss my cheek and whispers, "You look like my little boy, you look like a son."

LETTING GO

I am on the beach a cold winter Sunday, dressed in white jeans, white t-shirt, white blazer. My feet are bare. The sand is unusually clean, shells are arranged in tribal patterns of the sun and moon, man and woman. I can't recall if these designs had appeared there with the tide or were there from when I arrived. I feel something move in my hand, which I grip tightly, a thick sea-worthy rope woven of twine. The length moves away from me like a kite's string. I can see the other end is tied to my old lover's foot in the wing tips he used to wear when he worked. The soles have been worn down. My old lover's arms move spastically, as if holding his balance on a current I can't visualize. He looks down at me like I am the angel. We haven't had sex in over a year; he has been in this condition for quite a while.

My new lover, Rudy, is at my elbow, trying to pull me away with his usual arguments. We haven't had sex either. Not that Rudy hasn't tried, rubbing his crotch on the side of my leg, kneeling in front of me, unzipping my fly till I nearly fumble with the rope. Today he has been shopping, and is wearing the sheer white bathing suit he purchased. The trunks are skin tight, "Versace" runs along the waistband in bold black letters. Rudy turns around like a model, gold fleurs-de-lys are on each cheek of his ass.

There are moments when I want to get rid of this rope, having tested how many fingers I can actually let go of and still be able to manage the rope. The smaller fingers feel dead or asleep. As they curl open I can see cuts and bruises inside my palms. Rudy has brought astringent because he knows it will sting, and arnica because it can heal. I tell him that it doesn't hurt, but he refuses to hear that, insists that I should let go as he holds onto the rope himself. He says there are rolls of bandages he can wrap around my hands. I see through his deception. "How are you going to be able to hold the rope and bandage my hands?"

It's when I lose my temper that the priests come waltzing in. It has happened before. Their faces are drawn, skin and bones. The father today is particularly ugly, lesions cover what little flesh is exposed, his breath smells of shit and urine. He looks close in my face, says, "Son, it is time to let go, last rites, you need to live in the city of God." My old lover smiles, unaware of what is being said around me. He is so trusting. He has given Rudy and me his blessing, has thrown down what was left in his pockets, a brass lighter, copper coins as gifts to us. Rudy holds on to them, has buried them somewhere farther upshore.

I look where I believe the artifacts are buried and can see the sand rises in little dunes. I notice a head growing out of the sand, a young woman with long, black hair. My mother at sixteen. A young man follows her, reaches to hold her hand. By that simple touch, magic, I see her belly swell. There is pain in her eyes, regret for being so young. When I am born, my father dances with me in his arms, drunk. I smell his love. My mother pulls me away from him. He begins to strangle her, she won't leave. I want to ask her why, she slaps me. My neck feels broken and she continues to hit me. I grab her hand. I am now grown, masturbating every day in the bathroom, letting the water run to cover the sound. My mother is afraid of what I can do to her. I am sure of my strength, my ability to break her arm. That's when she tells me what a handsome boy I've become. My father turns his back on us, the muscles in his back are knotted. All he says is, "Faggot." My mother wants to hit me but cannot bring herself to do it. I see myself walk away from them alone.

It's like a mirror grazing over the sand, moving quickly to confront me. I try to have Rudy look at my life, but he is biting at my ear, blowing warm air into the canal. His fingertips are warm as they move over my body. I turn back to my image, now standing in front of me. Rudy says he is going to leave if I don't let go. As he moves away I gradually become colder. I hand the rope to my image, which he gladly accepts, seems to have strength I have lost. It is the first time I have ever released the rope and my hands feel strange and useless. Rudy is near, running down the beach. My image is being dragged into the ocean. I start running for Rudy, but I can't take my eyes off myself. I yell out my new lover's name. He stops. I look back and see my image drowning in the ocean, my old lover looks more like a dead fish floating in an aquarium. Rudy kisses me, says, "Today . . ." and can't complete his thought. The water has completely covered my image and the rope seems to have lost all tension. I return to Rudy, unsure that I love him or that I even want to be with him. I look down at my feet gliding over the sand, notice the cuffs of my pants have begun to fray, the threads twirl in the sea air and start to become twine.

SIGHT

At first I think it must be the fires and the winds, miniscule ash floating through the air and into my eyes. Or the dry Santa Anas pushing down the hillsides, raising the temperature till moisture vanishes, making the edges of my eyes blood red. On the freeway, driving to my doctor, I see clouds of black smoke billowing off the mountains, strange aerial formations of crows and seagulls, twisting and turning like a swath of fabric falling in air. These are the signs, clues written in some ancient script, and I want to know what it all means. The doctor looks at me, her hair pulled back away from her face, as if she were asking,

"Can't you read this language?" She is obviously frustrated, her fingers snap against each other, disbelief in their sounds. I must look ridiculous, sitting there, a smile across my mouth. She pulls out a model of a large eye the size of a bowling ball. She begins to disassemble the eye, the cornea, the retina, the optical nerve. I push the parts away from me; I can see that everything, everyone in her office has a glow around their bodies, some with colors more distinct, others thin and wavering. Even more unsettling, some people leave trails of light, a residue that takes a long time to dissipate. Occassionally a trail will curl upward, a large snake the color of ochre, poised as if ready to attack any nearby person. The doctor wants me to understand, says without this medication there is no hope; without this medication you are sure to lose all the sight that you have; the small discomfort you'll experience will be worth it compared to the alternative; what is one more drug to you? She is telling the truth, I can see it being said in the gold light that temporarily covers her body, can taste it under my tongue like a hazelnut liqueur. I tell her, "No, thank you." That is all I have to say and she starts shaking her head. The bones in her neck pop; she tells me I am foolish. By the time I near home, the drive has become more dangerous. My peripheral vision diminishes, the crest of my forehead, the crown of my head seems to ignite. My other senses revel in new-found power, guiding me through a maze of streets, using the scent of jacarandas and freshly cut, large-leaf philodendrons, the feel of bumps on the road, the dampness along my arm that means I've come into my underground parking space. People seem entranced with me as I step into the lobby of my apartment building; there is vague recognition but no recall of my name. I hear a few whisper, "Who?" They look at me as one would a religious painting, a lamentation. I am temporarily blinded by the various colors spewing out from their bodies, can see one man is covered with nothing more than white static, while another woman has tendrils of bluish light connected to everyone she's near. For a moment the inside of my chest seems hollow. I smile briefly; by now I am used to people not recognizing me because of weight loss, the waste of my muscles, but this is different. An elderly woman holds the elevator for me, her arm braced against the closing door. A warm tingle runs down my throat, informs me that she is not well, some perceived similarity with myself. I face her and smell lavender, old wool, sweat like eucalyptus oil. Her hair is white, I know, but I see tumors instead, the stench of black rotted fruit, dappling her brain. Her heart is erratic and I feel as if it is my own and that I am the one who will fall soon. I want to touch her. I sense the elevator aching to lift us up. She is saying something to herself, I hear her say the word "God" with the warm buzz of bees and wooden flutes in her mouth. I feel my palm near her shoulder and her body begins to change, slippery as mercury. Now I can see an amber light emanating from her stomach, her head. She is unsure of why she feels better, but she takes it like a gift of inestimable worth. In my room I lie back, close and open my eyes and all is darkness. My ears hum, and the woolen blanket beneath my fingers seems unbearably rough. For a second I think I have fallen asleep, and now it is late, the street lights are turned off. Somewhere in the house, my roommate watches TV. Miles away I can sense my folks readying themselves for sleep, the rustle of their bedsheets, the sounds they make using the bathroom. My brother far away in another state begins to open a can of beer; I hear him spray the fluid across his hand. It used to make me sick, the thought of my family, but now I see it as a legacy I will not understand till much later. Through the window, a man watches me: he is white, bright as if a hundred candles were burning inside him. He sees that I am ready, calls more of his people to the window. At first I pretend not to know what he offers, can taste meat in my mouth, blood on my lips. There is no judgement on whatever I do; he is just there for me. Before I go, I want to tell my roommate what he needs to take to stay alive, the astragalus I have in my closet, this new experimental treatment out of Korea. I want to call my ex-lover and explain that I really understand why he had to leave me, his heart battered like bronze from all the other deaths in his life. I want my mother to know I know where all her anger comes from, and if I could just touch a certain spot on her body, near her breastbone, it would all be released, she would always be warm after that. But I have come to the end, thoughts of the world seem woven of thread, thinly disguised, a veil. I let the angels consume me, each one biting into my body, until nothing is left, nothing but a small glow and even that begins to perish.

2

TO THE FIRST TIME

As if everything special was marked holiday,
the cold night air made strange
by mask and costume, hoof and sequin.
A feast day on Santa Monica Boulevard,
drag on Halloween. Voices crowded the corners,
bustle to bustle and I was still a virgin watching
nervous-eyed, the bare-chested men act out Pan.

Even his name was exotic, Emerson, Southern
in root, a loose drawl. I admired his tongue.
We stood in the Revolver's door frame.
the bar pumped up like a heart over-burdened
and in his blue suit he conveyed ease.
It was easy to hand over innocence,
all it took was him asking.
I could have fallen there already, his chin's bristle,
the bite of his teeth, his lips, autumn's chapped effect.
He laid it all on the bed's head table, alongside candles,
incense burners, the Welch's and vodka in tumblers.
His patience, the fingers lubricating parts of my body
I denied existed, kept under wrap by briefs and jeans.
When he told me to turn over, I did, trusted
his chest on my back, his legs separating mine,
winced at the pressure of pain.
It's rare, he said later, to be able to do it the first time,
to allow the muscles to relax and accept this pleasure.
A ragged towel on his lap, a swirl of jism

hooked inside a hair's curl, his thigh damp from himself.
He wanted to protect me from the things out there,
ready to hurt, hands explaining, pointed at the white paste,
a danger already prevalent, my desire to dab it on a finger
when he turned, to swallow the treat,
my belief, love could never be harmful,
that nights would last forever.

DEAR RICHARD

little did I know that we'd both grow up queer
back in 3rd grade. I was such a bully-faggot.
The humiliation you endured.
Even on Sunday, our first steps towards communion,
you avoided my attention like sin after mass.
Eyes shadowed, being dragged by your father's hairy fist,
you looked down at the asphalt, the church shoes mingled.
Back at school, morning ritual was the boy's restroom
and I always made you late, made you do Mae West,
big wrists bent on jutted hips. "Why don't you come up
and see me sometime? Is that a pistol in your pocket?"
If you didn't do what I said, I pulled your pants down
forced you to walk around school, underwear to ankles.
I only did it once, in an empty stall. You were pure white,
clean as porcelain, your penis a faucet handle
out of antique history. I had to stare, have a closer look
on my knees, a growth of hair already sprouted at your base.
A topographical map, I wanted to press in the gradient
mountains, scratch the cradle of land, trace the blue river
veins, the Tigris, Euphrates, and drink.
It was natural to have you inside my mouth, like a straw
    in milk,
fights after school and too naive to know what's shame.

It's hard to live in this same city. The apologies I make
every time I've run across your whereabouts, hear Mae West.
I see you at the bars, on the streets, even at the Gay

parade,
I look down wondering what you tell people, if you
were raped
or if it was your first blow job? I hope you believe me
when I say I'm sorry, that I've tried to reconcile
those years, whether I should feel remorse or pride
at knowing what I wanted so young, and taking it as if
by right.

MY FATHER NEAR RETIREMENT

His patio blooms with impatiens,
star-shaped succulents,
freshly painted lattice,
feeders of sugar, water and seed.
He is close to the ground, small shovel and rake.
Dad combs through camelia roots like hair,
the way he used to tame the mop on my head,
just before mass.
He tells me he no longer wants to work
on Saturdays or Sundays,
that the brewery will get along without him,
there are others who can fix the machines.

I know his fingers kill him.
Grease under the nails,
years of turning bolts
bare-handed, the strength we kids knew
he possessed, every time he flexed
his bulldog tattoo growled,
leashed under the sleeve of his t-shirt.
But he'd never hit any of us.
There wasn't time. He had to work.
Godlike he'd appear by our beds, after the bar,
drop coins and pocket fuzz near our pillows,
a kiss to wake us up.
I'd pretend to stay asleep,
watch him grab onto the wall,

lean on something more sturdy than himself,
afraid his fuddled moves could cause earthquakes
or other disasters.

It's a hobby, he says, dusting
the dirt off his pants, this new world
lush with budding fruit, a chaise longue,
Italian ceramics filled with apples.
He wears sweaters, fingers remove old leaves;
he's surprised by a clusters of grapes,
miniature and sharp in flavor.
"The vine is only a year old!"
His lips turn the color of burgundy.
I can see that he has pride
in all that has come up and grown,
furrows around his eyes,
a skill to nurture.
It thrives in this soil,
the stock of his hard work
earth the color of his children's children's
skin, and he lives on.

BORDERTOWNS

for L.A.

1.

The wind is a black bird
in her hair, long
as the fresh asphalt drive
to San Diego/Tijuana.
Laura's arms are crossed
to sleep, her body
vibrates from the road.

Before we left,
still parked in the driveway,
I said a prayer out of habit
not to get lost or separated.
Now I watch her,
wild strands whip over lashes,
eyes covered by dark glasses.
I roll up the window.
She starts,
tries to place where she is.
The ocean laps at her door,
the border combs the land.

2.

She looks for velvet paintings,
onyx eggs, blankets of pale blue,
pale pink. I am a few feet ahead
peering into glass cabinets,
silver braclets, hoops, charms.
We hardly speak to each other
but I turn back to see she's there.

The vendors think we are married
the way she snaps at me,
"Look," or "How about this?"
The men show me pallets of wedding rings,
women offer bridal gowns all in white lace.
I know she's laughing as hard as I am,
she finds it difficult to imagine
anything but a woman's body next to hers.
We settle for a polaroid on the burro cart,
put on ponchos and sombreros.
In cocky letters, my brim spells
"Cisco Kid." and Laura sparkles,
"Kiss Me."

RESURRECTION

Cross bound on black wooden beams,
the ropes are coiled around my wrists.
He is vigilant,
encased in Roman skin and hood.
His gloves rub my thighs
to see if I still kick.
I am carved with his name.

And these are the dangers:
the jackknife, the mouth,
the wing-shaped muscles of the back,
the sudden loss of weight
till nothing is holding me down,
just bones and leather,
the scars of being eaten alive.

THERE ARE PLACES YOU DON'T WALK AT NIGHT, ALONE

1.

Whittier Blvd., Beverly, Atlantic,
over by Johnson's Market,
or the Projects on Brooklyn.
There weren't any Bloods
or Crips yet on TV and everyone
bought bandannas
at Sav-on. Combinations
of blue and red packages,
the cellophane crinkled in the hand.
I wore them quartered
in my back pocket,
loose as a hanky.
The *cholos* pulled wool
beanies low,
just above their eyes,
warm and brown.
They'd cuff me from behind,
their hands lingering on my neck, saying
"Come here faggot, kiss me."
Their shoes made me crawl,
black mirrors, pointed tips,
Imperials that my lips fell upon
and leather soles
that brushed the hair out of my face
nearly blinding me.

2.

Manzanita, Hoover, Del Mar,
The Detour's After Hours.
I told him you had to walk
with an attitude.
Leather isn't thick enough
for a Buck knife
or a Corona
bottle, its end
jagged, twisted into
a washboard stomach.
Marc's t-shirt turned red,
the paramedics wouldn't touch him.
I filled in the holes,
my fingers adding pressure
on a hunter-green bandanna.
It changed to black,
warm in my hands.
His eyes were open,
his face rolled in my lap.

3.

Marengo, Arroyo, Colorado.
I walk like a policeman
to the bus bench
and some homeboys are waiting.
One has his shirt off
and his tattoo back reads,

"Viva La Raza."
They notice the fags going
into the white glass door
of the Adult Books and Films.
They see the pale limbs extended,
the shallow cheeks spotted,
the pink bandannas folded like
their own blue. They want to go in
but they're afraid they'd bleed.
The one-eighty rolls up
and they sit together
knees touching
corduroy against Levi's.
Brilliantine falls from their hair,
Three Roses, onto the hot vinyl seats.
My leather jacket creaks.
I want to smash them into the windows,
make them spread their legs,
my boots kicking them wide,
let my spit drip
into their ears,
seep into their brains,
tell them how much I love them.

THE BREATH OF GOD THAT BRINGS LIFE

for K.M. with devotion

. . . Saying it then,
against what comes: *wife*,
while I can, while my breath,
each hurried petal
can still find her.
— Raymond Carver

The heels of Kevin's palms massage my back
guide my head upward till I watch the ceiling.
It feels as if my bones could snap as twigs
the loss of spirit, the loss of breath,
but faith I put in my lover's hands,
his strength not to show fear when I am fearful.
Folded over a chair, ribbed oak
against my chest, I am lungs newly cleared
the process of gallium[†] infusions, respite.
Up close tiny fissures run across the grain.
I moan.

It's Friday, his bedroom, the first real rain,
the sound of the orchard, the garden,
drops on thick green leaves
avocados, plums, the more delicate grapefruit.
Inside, water seeps along the slatted windows,
a rivulet forms, stains gray the walls.

Kevin kneads between neck and shoulders,
thumbs roll down the spine like furrows.
I give in to his pressure, tension released.
His face gives nothing away but the job at hand,
small victories we've coaxed from my body,
a garden he has worked during war.
Again I moan.
He asks, "Did you say something?"

"Past the trees, can you hear it?"
A man is in the rain,
" . . . *alluhu akbar, laillaha illala* . . . "
a muezzin calls noon prayer,
Kevin repeats the rhymes of his words,
says this day, this hour is Jumma.*
He offers a crisp, blue Qur'an,
gold leaf pressed into leather, a flower.
I cherish its weight with free hands

and struggle for more air, chest held for a long moment
as if I had a lot to say,
"Honey."
Remember when I could not just a week ago
inhale fully,
birch leaf, golden seal tea.
Now I explode, muscles surrender to peace,
Kevin's flushed palms,
recall a dead man's poem
a wedding vow made of simple things:

water,
prayer,
breath.

---

†Gallium: A chemical injected for purpose of a gallium X-ray, used to detect PCP pneumonia.

*Jumma: Islam's holy day, Friday, especially noon prayer.

TURMOIL

Night after pungent night
we sweat, march through the city
hard and fast, unable to catch our breath.
Our bodies strike against each other,
shoulder to shoulder.
We could throw sparks up the dry hills,
Silverlake, LAX, the 101 ignited.
Thousands spurred by Sparklet's drums and bullhorns.
Our chrome whistles gleam under the moon,
children watch from bedroom windows,
some flip us off.
My lover and I are driven to sex now
four, five times a week.
I rub his moist, sore back,
the sweat lubrication,
tension removed from skin and sinew.
I admit I want to get belted,
parts of my body chewed,
to be told how I taste.

His chest I've shaved bare,
sharp razor, mentholated foam.
I treat his skin like a young boy's.
He lets me drift into sleep,
his pulse curls up along my back.
I imagine fire past the curtains,
a steady stream of molted earth,

rocks thrown through windows.
I kick away the sheets,
his arm is pressed around my waist
as if to never let go.
I want God to see this, unhindered,
what he created,
the mingle of flame and brawn
to smell the muscles of this love.

AT RISK

It's just after Christmas
and the waiting room is filled
with artificial limbs,
bulbs that twinkle,
packages wrapped
empty as rattles.

I am slouched by the exit
and the X-mas cards
are taped to the wall,
horses in the snow,
doves in the air.
A Black woman scolds her boy
all nerves and cough.
She tells me it's the flu,
tugs at his rough collar,
patches of hair
are missing from his head.

He runs to touch the tree,
the balsa nativity,
the paint-chipped ornaments,
his face reflecting large and round.
To her, he breaks everything nice.
She threatens him
with a rolled up magazine,
an ancient *Life*

or a *Woman's Day,*
the material my mother would read
and beat across my back,
poke me in the chest
till I hid far into the closet,
her dark dresses hanging over my head
and promises of burning my hands
on top of the stove.

The boy's arms fly
covering his head and neck,
his small elbows
against her sharp paper.
She looks at me
and I look at my watch
knowing it's my appointed time,
I've been waiting all week for the results.
The nurse calls out my name
and the little boy thinks they want him.
He hugs his mother's leg.
She just pushes him off
with her other foot,
lynches him by the string
around his jacket's hood,
the windbreaker at his throat.

I am asked to wait inside the doctor's office
meant to impress with diplomas,
pictures of him and Tom Bradley,

the choking sound of an aquarium.
I am just like any other queer,
I've sucked down enough come
to know that I'm infected.
The doctor thumbs my folder,
looks like my father behind those glasses,
and I hold back my tears.
He runs his hands down my neck
like a lover, checking for swollen glands
and even for this he wears gloves.
I nod when he says, We assumed you would be.
The chair next to me is empty.

The doctor leads me through the corridor
to the reception area, where all hell breaks.
The little boy scatters underneath the seats
and scented branches.
She hunts him down with her nails
and the air is cracked
by the sound of her hand slapping
the boy's cheek.
I can hear her sucking teeth,
"Do you want me to get the belt?"
She knocks him down to the floor.
The boy refuses to cry, knowing
she can really give him something to cry about.
He doesn't give any lip.
The doctor moves on
to other rooms, other patients.

I didn't dare ask how long I've got,
palm over my mouth,
I say mother
softer than I ever did before.

EVEN MONTHS AFTER THE DEATH, JOHN DREAMS

John tosses as if burned then drowned,
sweat and dampness,
a fever made from sex. His sharp-tongued lover
licks under his arms,
John's wrists held above his head
as if by rope, or the sheer force of the man's grip.
The dream's bedroom, lit by seven gold lamps,
makes the edges dark and captive.
Blood is there again, it rushes out of the wound
and his lover always laughs at John's horror,
twists his body, cups the fluid in his palms,
offers the rich wine, adoringly, the salty flavor of memory.

It was grief's cruel trick, to see his lover's face only in sleep.
John knew he'd never make love to him again,
the betrayal of the body, consumed under a simple shroud.
There wasn't a box of ash, a lock of hair,
or even a dirt mound to remember him by.
There was just John's hate of all people living.
And if he dared to interpret dreams,
he would cast anyone on a bed of suffering,
herald like a trumpet the beginning of plague,
mark others like beasts, to bring his beloved back into
the world.

THE QUILT SERIES

1. 911

I couldn't stay to take care of him,
and when I came home, John was delirious,
huddled into the corner of the couch,
the floor heater pinged loudly,
the pilots turned all the way up.
He sat trying to light cigarettes,
one after another,
his fingers acting as matches.
For days I forced him to eat,
begged him to sleep.
When the ambulance came
two swarthy men in open shirts,
snakes wrapped around an emblem,
yelled at me about drug overdose,
ransacked our one bedroom place,
saw the Honcho magazine
pages of cocksuckers in body chains.
They passed eyes at each other
knowing we were fags
and slipped on rubber gloves
and protective face gear.
John cried at everything happening to him
as they picked him up roughly by the arms,
his striped blue robe coming apart,
revealing ribs, feverish flesh

and balls swinging violently.
I kept on trying to close the terry cloth sides
re-tie the cords down the stairs
while his toenails dragged on the cement.
He swore that he hated me,
that he could never trust me again.
The men threatened him with a straightjacket,
"Calm down John or we'll have to use it."
I was Judas kissing him away
pulling the last restraints on the stretcher.
The guards pushed me back to the pavement
filled with the neighbors staring, hypnotized
by John's screams of murder
and the spinning red lights.
I was at their mercy
the doors closing my sight,
left to drive myself
to follow alone.
I choked down what was still inside,
put the key in the ignition
and turned over dead
when the engine finally started.

2. ICU

It was too easy to lie back in the chair
and just touch the tips of his fingers
like he was lost already,
death was dreaming.
I had never seen him sleep like this before
his face turned from mine,
lips torn and red,
an i.v. barbed into his vein.
Every other hour a young nurse would fly by,
draw blood, smile at me
as if I was a good boy to be so quiet,
so cooperative.
I had to remind myself
the virus in the brain was the enemy
as John's wrists jerked his restraints.
I'd walk to the cafeteria
and the big electric doors would swing for me
as if I was a VIP.
Alone at a plastic table
I would breathe on my coffee to cool,
listen to the others speak the Latin of medicine,
the curves of chance.
My future was planned: when he dies,
I will go home, drink a glass of milk,
pull a razor from the box,
drag it across the lines in my palms
up through the crooks of my arms.
It will be clean, it will be over.

Back in John's room, dressed in a gown,
I was an actor for friends, a tissue paper mask.
I told them the recent, He had a CAT scan.
He had a spinal tap.
They might put him on a respirator,
but I'm hopeful.
Everyone wanted to touch me,
ask me how I was holding up
if I needed anything,
their voices deadpan,
their hands, talc-lined gloves.
I stared out the window,
the sun rising strong.
I said what I wanted to see most were flowers,
get-well cards, a heart filled
with foil-wrapped chocolates,
their edges sharp as blades.

3. REM

As if shaken, he opened his eyes,
lucid and blue.
For a moment I thought the worst was over,
that we would round up his belongings,
his robe, the winter hyacinths,
a menu for a memory
and I would forget that I covered my mouth
from breathing his air,
touched him only with gloves,
ran into the other rooms for one clean glass.
John looked about, absorbing the metal pads
taped to his chest, his wrists wired down,
his waist tied to the bed.
He pulled with withered arms taut,
his mouth twitched in panic.
He stared at me till I was shame-faced.
His look said, "How can you do this?"
And I released the locks under the bed,
I told him it would take a minute
to check him through
but he was busy, pulling cords
off the pulse, the pressure points
and the monitor's lines went flat.
The nurses came running while he tore his i.v.
ripping the skin. He kept on screaming, "No
I don't want to die, I don't want to die,
I don't want to die!"
They were on top of him

like white ghosts ready to bury him,
stretching limbs and I watched his hand
strike for mine, pleading for help.
With knuckles and claws
they wrenched his right arm,
tapping for a good, strong vein.
They packed him with ice,
up his arm, between his legs,
below his neck
and he burned all night,
one hundred and five.
When the sweat stopped pouring,
I swept the curtains shut,
dropped the straps to the sides
began to rub his welts smooth.
He didn't notice me there,
my eyes moving over the bones of his shoulder,
my arms folded into a pillow,
wanting to curl inside his body
and the nights when he couldn't sleep without me.

4. RM#

John was constantly moved
and each time I returned,
I had to find the station
to find the room,
the hallways were endless.
Friends cried and strangled the corridors.
I ignored their open arms,
it made me mad when they held me back
so I'd push them away,
tell them, He looks great.
You should have seen him yesterday.
They wiped their faces unbelieving,
their fingers wrenched the flowers.
I felt like they should die instead,
not John, cornered to the wall, unconscious,
a halo of bare fluorescence.
I explained all the injections and wires
because I needed a distraction
from John's sunken face,
his bones that poked through skin,
his mind taken over by a fungus
his lips bloody from dehydration,
his tongue cracked and smeared
and a plastic tube shoved down his throat
taped to his mouth
and he was choking,
his veins collapsing,
his brain boiling,

his lungs filling with fluids
and the chemicals made him hallucinate
but they killed.
He slipped in and out
his hands fluttered, blessing the air.
I held down his arms,
strapped them to the metal rails
as if that would give me peace,
the one thing I prayed.
But all he could do was pick at my palm
pull at the false skin of latex,
stare past me like an animal who avoids the eyes.
Still I tried to whisper sweet thoughts into his ears,
"Baby I'm at your side, I love you so much,
I don't know what I'll do."
The nurses scattered the onlookers
till I was alone, suffocating.
I was told all I could do was go home and wait,
so I slept in our bed,
pulled his pillow to my face,
dreamt of when our bodies were covered
by the same white sheet.
By the next morning he was gone
and I spent what seemed like a day
chasing him down, out of breath,
his room unlisted, his name erased.

5. 4AM

I slept in my shirt,
smelled of sweat, drenched the bed.
I couldn't tell if the dampness
was from him or me,
I wouldn't change the sheets till he came home.
John was in a coma, his brain half-eaten.
The doctors said it was a matter of time,
they didn't know if he could hear me or not.
The phone rang,
crumbled any thought of dreams.
I pulled the voice off the cradle,
the nurse said, You better come over right away,
with a friend, don't hesitate, don't drive yourself,
promise me that. And I did.
Mike is closest, so I called him,
told him, I think this is it.
I was surprised by how cold I was,
gathered all the things I needed
a comb, a hankerchief,
the red sweater, the one he loves,
the one he bought me for my birthday.
My arms slipped through the heavy knots
and it seemed like hours since I called
but it had only been minutes.
In those minutes I'd relived our first kiss,
his arms around me
and the small ceremony
where we exchanged rings

and he gave me mine in a box,
wrapped inside another,
five in all. Five smooth years
enough to make my parent's silver marriage
feel wooden.
I bent the blinds and waited,
cursed myself for daring to leave his side.
The nurse called back, jolted me out of my skin.
She said she was sorry, but John passed away
at five minutes till four. I told her no.
She told me everyone was pulling for him.
Damn it you're wrong, he can't be dead.
All she could say was she was sorry,
so very sorry, if there's anything . . .
It's all right, there's nothing.
Slowly I hung up the phone,
felt my blood become glass,
my hands breaking my fall.
I knocked the ceramic birds off a shelf,
smashed my face into the doorjamb, again and again.
Later on people said time will heal,
but the pain was too much to forget,
his life pounded out of my head
and all that was left of mine,
measured from that point,
4AM sharp and I began to howl.

6. DOA

The bedsheets were drapery around his body.
John's hands were in the linen's folds,
a towel covered his waist.
Only weeks before, I was on my knees,
my face on his stomach,
feeling his breath
and the soft, blond hair
that led from the navel down.
I stared at him on the hospital bed,
his lips bruised by his teeth,
a crust of blood on his mouth.
I wanted to kiss him
but I was afraid of what I'd taste.
I locked my fingers into his hand
like a young lover's grip.
Still he felt more like meat than flesh.
I wanted to throw it down,
push him out of the bed,
I started telling him, I'm sorry I wasn't here,
I'm sorry it wasn't me.
Even this didn't wake him,
his eyes swollen shut,
patches of blue under his skin.
I began to comb his hair,
tuck the blanket to his chin.
I wanted to drag him home,
make him show me where the Christmas ornaments were
and his grandfather's watch,

the one his family wants back.
The weight of his hand slipped from mine
and I could see the scars across his arm.
When I got home, I expected him
to be in the front room, on the couch,
book in his lap, a fantasy.
Instead the curtains were still open
and the dull rain tapped on the window
bounced off the jade plant.
That night, I turned off the floor heater,
the blue flames vanished,
the whole house was cold.
I shivered in our bed,
his pillow between my legs,
his gold ring pulse
at the bottom of a drawer.
It died when I got up to touch it.

CONQUERING IMMORTALITY

for Marcus Antonio

Down on Hollywood Boulevard,
past the McDonalds,
between Numero Uno Pizza
and the boarded-up Ernesto's restaurant
lies a ruin.

In its time,
the Egyptian
was a palace,
a movie temple.
Cast heads of pharaohs
greeted at the entry doors,
while twin Dogs of Anubis
guarded the lobby filled
with lotus-capital columns,
Tut mask wall sconces
and hieroglyphs.

I remember
before I got sick,
my blood thin
and unable to clot,
before the time of lovers' funerals
and we only used first names
on their quilts —

John,
David,
Marc;
the Egyptian
was a derelict theater.
It had already amassed into three screens
and much of the ornamentation removed.
Eviscerated.
I came down to Hollywood
to see a movie,
started my journey at the Chinese,
made sure my steps didn't land
on any star's name
because I had respect
for the Walk of Fame.
I just turned 21.
This black man
standing at the corner of Highland
watched me coming down the street.
I waited for the red light
and he came up behind me
next to my ear,
made a loud slurping noise.
I could feel his tongue long and wet.
I turned to face him.
He was big,
about a foot taller than me,
hands enormous.
One rubbed a gold ankh across his chest

while his other hand grabbed between muscular legs.
Again he made this slurping sound
looked me down, then up.
I started to walk across the street
taking larger steps,
turning only when I got to the other side.
There I could see him,
this shit-eating grin across his face.

At that time
I was jacking-off regularly
to fantasies of getting screwed by men,
straight men,
their wives in bed with us
in pink, furry nightgowns.
The husband and I
would simply forget the woman
and when I was about to come
it would just be him and me.
I would sleep in the curve of his arm,
the sinews of his bicep,
a son wrapped in his father's protection,
as if masculinity
could save me.

During the Third Dynasty
Egyptians began to preserve corpses
from putrefaction,
removing their entrails

most liable to decay.
Motivated by fear,
they believed the deceased could come back to life,
so they built elaborate tombs
stocked with food and drink,
an offering table laden with goose and calves heads,
bread and flowers,
all to keep the dead in their place.
To produce a semblance of life in the after-life,
the embalmers' efforts were limited to placing cloth
soaked in resin on the body,
shaping it into human form.
The nose, mouth
external genital organs
were all faithfully molded.
The mummy of King Dedkare
has survived,
in a bad state
but nevertheless
retains scraps of skin, muscle,
tendons, ligaments,
blood-vessels,
nerves.
Inside, traces of resin on ribs
testify to the attention of the embalmers
as do the canopic jars near the body.

The man followed me into the theater,
the movie just about to start.
I leaned back into my chair,
my arms behind my head
like wings.
I stared into the ceiling
waiting for the lights to dim.
Above a large scarab
whose grilled wingspan
graced the entire dome
dominated my attention.
In school I had learned
that the scarab represented
the daily course of the sun,
its hind legs pushing a ball of cow dung.
As the light from the ceiling diminished
I felt the man sit next to me,
his arm pressing next to my own,
his leg rubbing up rhythmically against mine.
There was the sound of film
being taken up by the reel,
the blank beginning of scratched
lead tape, the stereo kicking in
and my own breath,
then his.

There is an episode
of the Twilight Zone,
that always runs in my head.

Ann Blythe played an actress
who was being interviewed
by this young, handsome reporter.
She was a successful actress,
living lavishly,
pool and large garden,
taken care of by an elderly relative.
The actress wore a scarab amulet
and the reporter noticed it in all of her photographs.
The elderly lady who lived there
seemed to want to talk to the reporter,
to say something to him,
but the actress kept on interfering.
Finally the elderly woman
told the reporter
that she was actually
the daughter of the actress,
that the actress was much older than she appeared
and the scarab kept the woman young
and immortal.

The Egyptian theater's sisters
were the more famous
Grauman's Chinese,
and the demolished
Metropolitan
noted for it's Persian-inspired
concrete forms.
Even though the Chinese survives,

most of its beauty has suffered
compared to its original decor
of rare tropical trees,
water fountains dripping from lotus flowers,
a ceiling lantern that concealed
organ pipes.

The Egyptian has been closed
for a long time.
It happened suddenly,
the gates were just locked up —
but looking back
I can see its demise
like the progression of a disease,
how without warning
simple things
like white cells
are no longer enough.
Or you rub your neck muscles
and feel a knot of flesh
and it hurts
and it makes you tired
and you notice your tongue isn't as red as it should be
and you can't tell if you sweat in bed
because you have too many blankets
and you don't want to panic
but you've seen it before
with other people
and you call them

ask them
but they don't know
and you can tell they're annoyed
because this is like the hundredth time
someone has called them
trying to get information
telling them their symptoms
instead of going to doctors
and finding out that way.
The clues fly around
like letters blown from the marquee,
only decayed hieroglyphs,
words that make no sense.

The man invited me to follow him
into the bathroom stall,
enclosing us in painted papyrus reeds,
a river made in tile.
I asked him his name,
but he said it wasn't important
and undid my belt.
He made me stand on the toilet seat,
grabbed my hardening dick and balls
and stuffed it all into his mouth.
I had never let anyone touch my asshole before,
he made small circles, designs.
I could feel the edge of his fingernail
trying to press in. I thought I was going to come.
He then grabbed my hips and turned me around,

made me suck the finger he'd been using,
to get it real wet.
Inside his palms I noticed callouses,
yellow as an animal paw.
I could taste myself on his finger,
my spit coating past his knuckle.
He again placed it against my ass,
I couldn't loosen up.
He kept on saying, "Baby, ahh baby."
I looked at my short pants
down around my ankles,
could see that he was spraying his white come
all over the insides,
the material darkened where he shot.
The usher's hand was large and loud
banging flat on the door,
his face acne-scared and hair shorn.
He called us damned faggots,
as if this was all too common,
a look of tiredness across his mouth.
There were two other ushers
in the bathroom, bored
having to bust up another couple of fags
like nameless creatures fucking in plain sight
who needed to be shamed
and we begged for it.

Seth was a jealous god
and the brother of Osiris.

He had already tricked Osiris
into a jeweled coffin,
floated him off in the Nile.
Isis, the wife and sister of Osiris,
found him and brought him back to life.
Seth, enraged, dismembered Osiris
and scattered his remains
throughout Egypt.
Isis found all the parts
except the male organ
which was swallowed by a fish.
Osiris became the god of the dead.
In many inscriptions written on sarcophagi,
an invocation can be read,
"Greetings O thou art chief of the great . . .
I am Osiris."
All the dead become Osiris.

I've had to move into Hollywood
because it's closer to my doctors,
the food bank,
legal services
and I don't drive anymore
because I can't afford a car
on Social Security.
So I take the bus,
walk around a lot.
After the big earthquake
I went touring Hollywood,

surprised by how building facades
were leaning into the street,
how entire cornices,
murals of legendary stars,
store front windows were blown
onto sidewalks and gutters,
so much debris.
"The city is going to hell,"
an Evangelist yelled at me
through a bull horn,
"disease, riots, floods and fires, now this!"
"Repent!"
I shook my head
as if to shiver out
all his hatred xeroxed on a piece of paper
he tried to force into my hand.
We felt a small tremor
and both the Evangelist and I
took it as a sign
that God was on our side,
as if God could choose between his children,
as if he loved one more than the other.

I look like the city,
only bare bones of what I used to be,
shitting endlessly
no test,
no pill
can stop me from wasting,

the virus attacks my brain,
invades my spine and every organ,
my cock limp and floundering.
As if my death
would be a surprise.
I stop to turn around from the gated Egyptian,
can see the walls have broken
between bricks,
the roof apparently falling apart,
tiles strewn on the sidewalk.
Towards the back a great hole has opened,
while the adjacent wall
seems to have separated
and now leans outward.
There have been talks of saving the Egyptian before,
articles on its historical importance
of redevelopment.
Nothing more has been done.

As I enter my seventh year of diagnosis
where reports of anti-viral promise
and T-cell counts
have lost their assured importance,
I see my life as a series of facades,
each layer in erosion;
white patches along the sides of my mouth,
a shortening of breath,
a burning pain in my calves,
each taking an ability away from me,

to where keeping simple food down
is what is of value.
Forgotten is career and income,
no longer the depiction of my personality
but disabilities are what frame me.
And what is left
after my body, torn down,
is my soul.

I notice as I stand here
that today is beautiful,
that the sand-colored walls of the Egyptian,
yellow like dark mustard,
set out against this blue sky.
Along the roof line,
frescoed palm leaves
in azure, gold and blood red
look as vibrant
as if painted today.
The walls of this building
are sturdy like myself,
guarded by the spirits of long dead stars.
And even if the parapets are bulldozed in haste
this sacred space can never die out.
I steal underneath the chained gate,
enter through shattered lobby doors,
glass at my feet.
I grab the serpentine necklace around my neck,
green scarab the color of the Nile.

I am protected by myth,
a dream of immortality,
enfolded in this theater's
tomb-like darkness.

ABOUT THE AUTHOR

Gil Cuadros published stories and poems in *Indivisible, High Risk 2,* and *Blood Whispers.* His work is also on the compact disc, *Verdict and the Violence: Poets' Response to the LA Uprising.* He was awarded the 1991 Brody Literature Fellowship, and was one of the first recipients of the PEN Center USA/West grant to writers with HIV. He lived in Los Angeles until his death in 1996.